SINCE WE LOVE

SINCE WE LOVE

Denise Robins

CHIVERS

British Library Cataloguing in Publication Data available

This Large Print edition published by AudioGO Ltd, Bath, 2013.

Published by arrangement with the Author's Estate

U.K. Hardcover   ISBN   978 1 4713 3973 8
U.K. Softcover   ISBN   978 1 4713 3974 5

Printed and bound in Great Britain by TJ International Limited

CHAPTER ONE

Joan Parwood walked through the deserted lounge of the Great Friars Hotel, nodded good-morning to the yawning boy who was washing the stone steps outside the massive oaken door, and received the post which was delivered at seven o'clock every morning by a postman with a motor cycle and sidecar.

The sight of that red sidecar bearing the Royal Coat of Arms never failed to excite Joan. Not that she expected to hear from anybody in particular. But to her there was always something exciting about a postman with his mail bag. After all, one never knew what that bag contained, and it was fun imagining that there might be a love-letter, or an unexpected legacy; a thrill of some kind awaiting one in a small white envelope.

At this hour, Joan forgot to be the dignified manageress of an important riverside hotel. The 'Miss Parwood' on whose slim shoulders rested the responsibility of a big staff, and whose job it was to see that things ran on oiled wheels. The 'Miss Parwood' of whom the servants must go in awe, to whom the guests could complain and who must bear all the strain and stress of the management. And at the end, be able to satisfy her employer that she was running the place at a profit! A big job

1

for a girl of twenty-four.

Joan carried the post into her office and began to sort it. She hummed a little under her breath. She had nothing much to hum about, but it was her nature to be philosophical and thankful for small mercies. It was really a feather in her cap to hold down a job like this, with a salary of £200 a year and all expenses paid. Besides, Great Friars was one of the most beautiful and historic houses which had ever been turned into a hotel.

It was packed for the week-end, nearly always full during the summer months. And this was a perfect June morning. The sun streamed through the window on to Joan's desk. Outside, in the tangle of jasmine and honeysuckle creeping over the grey stone walls, the birds sang madly. It was the hour that Joan liked best. When the hotel guests were still sleeping, and except for the bustle of the staff, there was comparative peace.

The letters slipped through Joan's hands. She sorted them ready for pigeon-holing. Ah! A familiar one for herself. How well she knew that blue notepaper with the big, round, untidy writing, the crest on the flap of the envelope, and the West End postmark. From Sally Vaughan, owner of the hotel and Joan's 'boss.'

The note was brief and characteristic of Sally.

Dear Joan,
Expect me for lunch on Saturday. Simon's
driving me down and will also be staying
the weekend. Good news at last!
S.'

Joan folded the note, put it in the pocket of the tussore smock which she wore over her dress in the mornings when on duty, lit a cigarette and began to walk up and down the room restlessly.

So that's what the post had brought her this morning! The intimation of her employer's arrival—with Simon Roxley—and the promise of 'good news.'

Well, it was good news from only one person's point of view. Sally's. Joan knew what it meant. Simon had given way to Sally at last and consented to an early wedding.

There was no longer a song on Joan Parwood's lips, nor a song in her heart. And the morning no longer seemed golden or peaceful to her. She was thinking:

'How frightful! What on earth am I going to do? How am I going to get out of it all? Why must I go through all this pain?'

Somebody knocked on the frosted glass door.

At once the youthful, human Joan, full of warm impulses, sensitive, emotional, retreated behind the cool mask of the manageress. She took the cigarette from her lips and threw it out of the open window.

'Come in,' she said.

But it was not one of her staff as she had anticipated. A tall, fair man wearing grey flannels and a tweed coat thrust in a head and said:

'Hallo! Don't get the porter to throw me out. I'll go quietly.'

Joan relaxed.

'Oh, it's you! Good morning, Ham. Have you come for an early morning cup of tea?'

'If I can drink it with you and get it free of charge.'

Joan laughed and put a finger on the bell.

'I daresay the hotel will stand you that.'

'I want to be entertained by you, not the hotel,' he grumbled.

She sat down at her desk and returned to the task of sorting letters.

William Hamley, more often known to his friends as 'Ham,' balanced himself on the edge of the desk and looked tenderly down at the dark, graceful head of the girl. He never could regard Joan Parwood as the hard, business-like young woman who ran this hotel so efficiently. To him, she was just a kid and a very lovely one—much too lovely to be wasted in a job which kept her inside an office, in a still-room checking provisions, or a linen-room, dealing out laundry. It was a fine job and a grand spot for her to live in, but in Ham's opinion, Joan Parwood ought to be leading a more glamorous existence. There was so much glamour in her personality and appearance—for him, anyhow, and for a lot of other men, so far as he could judge.

He counted himself amongst her greatest admirers. He had proposed to her twice and been rejected, but that did not deter him. He was the owner and proprietor of 'Hamleys,' the biggest garage in the town, and did all the repairs for Great Friars, so he saw a great deal of the young manageress. Nothing suited him better. She had told him firmly that she could only be a friend to him, and like that things remained—not that Ham intended they should do so permanently. He was much too much in love. He was thirty and Joan was the only girl he had ever wanted to marry.

She finished sorting the mail, leant back in her chair and looked at him.

'What are you doing here at this ungodly hour?'

'Mr. Mathews wanted the Bentley. He said he was leaving here before breakfast on his way to Wales, so I thought I'd bring it round myself.'

'Well, as soon as our tea comes, I must leave you, Ham. We've got a crashing week-end in front of us. Full to overflowing.'

'Miss Vaughan coming down?'

'Yes.'

'Roxley with her?'

'Yes.'

5

Joan's head went down again. She busied herself by filling her fountain-pen. She was not anxious that Ham should see the colour which rose in her cheeks at the mention of Roxley's name. But the eyes of a lover are quick, and Ham saw that wildrose pink creep up under the girl's golden tan. He frowned and kicked a leg against the desk.

He was pretty certain that Joan was in love with Roxley. And what the hell's use was that when he was going to marry her boss? Of course, Joan had never said anything. But he was ready to stake his life that she was keen on the fellow. She always gave herself away by colouring at the mention of him. Ham didn't like it. He knew and admired Simon Roxley. He had had dealings with him several times over a car and had always found him a most charming, entertaining fellow. But there were rumours that he wasn't as much in love with Sally Vaughan as she was with him. Rumours, too, that it was half on account of the money behind Sally that he was marrying her. It might or might not be true, but everybody knew that the Roxleys were broke. And Simon's father, old Sir George, wanted him to save the family fortunes by marrying someone with cash.

Ham said abruptly:

'When are those two getting married?'

Joan's face remained hidden.

'Shortly, I should think.'

'Good job when they are.'

Then up came Joan's head quickly.

'Why?'

Ham's clear blue eyes—the redeeming feature in his blunt, boyish but unhandsome face—looked straight into the bright hazel of hers.

'They've been engaged long enough, haven't they?'

'Only six months.'

'That's long enough. I think the thrill is apt to go out of a marriage when a couple hang round months and years before they're tied up.'

'Maybe.' Joan's reply was non-committal.

Ham continued almost aggressively:

'And I shouldn't be surprised if the thrill hasn't gone out of theirs. On his part, if not on hers.'

Again the hot surge of colour to Joan's face and throat, try as she would to destrain it. But the subject of that engagement was one that touched her so very deeply. So much more deeply than it ought to. She was thankful that one of the waiters interrupted them at this point by bringing in a tea tray.

But as soon as Ham received his cup of tea he harped back on the engagement, as though it was on his mind, too.

'Everyone who knows them seems to think she's much more in love with him than he is with her. I have a pal who knows the Roxleys very well and . . .'

'It isn't really our business, Ham,' broke in Joan rather sharply.

He slid off the desk.

'I'm getting the bird this morning.'

'Not really.' She was quick to mollify him for she was fond of Ham. A woman couldn't help it. There was something so nice and friendly about him always. And Joan knew in her heart that he must suffer over her at times. He was far from ready to accept her on platonic terms.

Sally Vaughan had told her last week-end that she was a little fool not to marry Ham. He had a big business. He was putting up other garages along the river. He came from a good family and had a Public School education. She would have a good time as his wife. There would be none of the slavery that she had to face here. And slavery it was in the busy season, for she was conscientious about her job. But she could not marry Ham, because she did not love him. And more than that. It was because she loved somebody else. And that somebody else was Simon Roxley.

The whole thing was a muddle and she had never felt more confused or miserable. She thanked heaven for the philosophic streak which was in her, and for hard work. When she was immersed in her job, it helped her to forget. But there wasn't much chance of forgetting when Simon Roxley came down and stayed in the hotel.

Ham was making things no better for her

by voicing what she knew in her heart to be true. Simon was not so much in love with Sally as she was with him. Joan almost wished that it were not so. Had she known that he was utterly devoted to Sally, she could more easily have conquered her own feelings for him. But to conquer them, knowing that Simon was not altogether happy about his engagement, remembering a certain moment, two weeks ago when she had danced with him at a party here, and that look in his eyes which no woman could mistake, was much more difficult. Of course it was madness to think about him at all or to remember anything. He was going to marry Sally. He couldn't possibly be interested in her, Joan. He mustn't be. That dance, that look . . . it had all been fleeting madness. A man's momentary reaction to feminine allure. Not that she flattered herself that she was so alluring. Neither had she meant to awaken his interest—that way. But she did attract men. There had been others besides Ham who had wanted her. And Simon Roxley found her sympathetic and had told her so. He liked to talk to her. That was always dangerous—to be the sort of woman a man likes talking to!

Sally wasn't that kind. She was much too voluble herself. She liked to do the talking. She was always gay and on the top of her form. A little overpowering at times, perhaps. Beautiful, spoiled, exacting, and out to get what she wanted in life. A man wouldn't find it easy to get away from Sally.

Did Simon want to get away from her? Had he regretted his proposal after that cruise down the Dalmatian coast with Sally and her father?

Joan did not know for certain, and did not want to know. It was much better that she shouldn't. It was too awful to be in love with somebody else's future husband. Especially when one had never been in love before. Joan had never found it easy to give her heart to anybody. But it had been wrung out of her by Simon Roxley; by something intrinsically appealing in his eyes, his smile, the tilt of his head, the lilt of his voice, the elusive, fascinating personality that was Simon's.

He had had a mesmeric influence on her from the very first day she had met him. A day to remember, when Sally had come back from her cruise, proudly bearing her fiancé with her. Proud, because she had got what she had schemed for, Simon, his future title, his fine old family name, his pride, in return for her money. She was in love with him, like most women who knew him. He had that effect upon them. But Joan Parwood was horrified because she, too, had allowed herself to be affected.

It had not disturbed her seriously until a month ago. For the last four or five months, Sally had come down at regular intervals with Simon to stay at Great Friars. The hotel was her hobby. One of the 'toys' that her father had bought her. And she had put Joan in to manage it because Joan was an old school friend. One of the few members of her own sex whom Sally really liked and admired. But the Parwoods were not well off and Joan had been left an orphan and had taken up hotel work while Sally was still doing a 'deb' season in town. It had been a lucky 'break' for Joan when her old friend had bought this place and got in touch with her and offered her the management.

Today, Great Friars meant less of a toy to Sally than in previous years. Her father gambled recklessly in a big way. The Vaughan fortune had received a few shocks this last year. A good deal of Sally's money was tied up in the hotel. Therefore, the profits were now of importance to her. She was delighted with the way Joan managed the place and looked after her interests. And until old Sir George died and Roxley Hall became Simon's and hers, Sally intended to live at Great Friars after her marriage.

It was a glorious old house, the glorious grounds with green lawns sloping down to the river. In Tudor times it had been a famous monastery. But today, in the great hall where once the monks had eaten, simply and sparingly, looking out of the mullioned windows at the river, fashionable crowds from Mayfair lunched and dined and danced.

11

Joan had grown attached to the place. The last thing she wanted to do was to hand in her resignation. But if she did not feel better about Simon once he was married to Sally than she did now, she would have no alternative.

She heard Ham's voice:

'You're doing a lot of thinking this morning.'

She wrenched her mind away from Simon.

'Well, my main thought now is to see the chef about menus for the day,' she said briskly.

'What a wise head on those little shoulders,' said Ham, and although he smiled, his heart ached a bit. He wished he were not so much in love with her. There was so much candour and sweetness in the hazel depths of Joan's large eyes, set exquisitely in the pure oval of her face. She wore her smooth, dark hair parted in the centre and knotted in the nape of her slender neck. She was not the ordinary 'pretty girl', but so much more, in Ham's estimation. She had a fine, tranquil beauty. And Ham knew there was fire and passion behind that serenity. It was there, in the warm red curve of her mouth. (If only it had been his lot to rouse that fire, he thought.) Except for a touch of lipstick, Joan used no makeup. She needed none, with those sweeping black lashes and pencilled brows.

He would like to have stayed talking, but she was not to be coerced away from her duty. So, a few moments later, he drove away back

12

to his garage, and Joan, with pad and pencil in hand, went forth to her first job of the day, her interview in the big kitchens with the head chef.

But while she listened to suggestions for soup, fish and entrée, it was not the thought of Ham that kept creeping between her and her job, but the thought of Simon Roxley. Simon, who was coming here today with her employer. Simon whom, she felt sure, she must congratulate on an imminent marriage. She was certain that the wedding date had been fixed.

Her heart kept repeating that cry of an hour ago:

'What am I going to do? Why must I go through all this pain?'

CHAPTER TWO

At one o'clock, a black and silver Mercedes-Benz rolled through the wrought-iron gateways leading into the grounds of Great Friars, and pulled up at the hotel entrance. The driver was a tall, thin girl dressed somewhat theatrically in white, with white fox furs and a flowered hat set jauntily on the side of a head which gleamed with platinum-fair curls.

She stepped out of the car, drawing off

white leather gloves. Her companion, an uncommonly tall, graceful young man in grey flannels, his black head uncovered, waited to light a cigarette before he got out.

'We have certainly arrived on a heavenly day, Simon,' said the girl. 'But am I longing for a drink? *I'll* say I am.'

Simon Roxley yawned. He disliked Sally when she used American slang and dressed herself like a Hollywood film star. Indeed, he was in one of his bad moods today. He was not one whit fired by Sally's looks, although she was lovely enough with her enormous blue eyes and dazzling fairness. She was nice, too. Gay, kind and generous. Oh! There was no limit to Sally's generosity. She had plenty, and all that she had, she wanted to give him. No girl on earth could be more anxious to help save the Roxley estates, put Simon on his feet, make it easy for him to live the extravagant sort of life he had always lived until taxation, falling investments, death duties, and one thing and another had brought his family to penury. And at moments, certainly, he was physically stirred by her. Or *had* been. Quite in love when he had asked her to marry him. He need not label himself as a swine who was merely after her cash. That cruise down the Dalmatian coast had been a glamorous affair. And he had found glamour in getting engaged to Sally Vaughan. Besides, it was a case of 'fifty-fifty'. She was in love with him and he had a title coming and a position which she coveted.

But that was all six months ago, and since then he had met Joan . . .

Simon Roxley's dark, narrow, brilliant eyes roved in utter discontent from his fiancée to the blaze of scarlet and yellow wallflowers fringing the drive, and on to the lovely grey Elizabethan house. A house which he had always felt was much too individual and romantic to have been turned into a modern hotel.

Joan was there . . . He would see her today, as he always saw her, much occupied, conscientiously performing her numerous tasks, doing a job as Sally herself could never possibly do one. Sally was born lazy.

Darling Joan! . . .

Why the devil had fate ordained that just when he had settled his life nicely with Sally, he should meet the one and only woman in the world?

Joan was that woman. He knew it. He had known it for several weeks now. Ever since that dance they had had together, when he had suddenly discovered the fragrance and allure of her and she had ceased to be the capable Miss Parwood and become just the girl of a thousand dreams.

He had tried ceaselessly to banish the thought of her. To deny her strong attraction for him. To remind himself that she was a

15

penniless young woman in a job, who would never be suitable for him. Added to which, he had not even spoken to her on the subject. For all he knew, she might have turned him down flat had he proposed to her. Yet, when he allowed himself to think about her, he was half-ready to swear that she was interested in him. Not only as the future husband of her employer, but as a man.

'Come on, Simon,' Sally called from the doorway.

The head porter and a boy, touching their caps respectfully, ran forward to lift the suitcases from the back of the Mercedes-Benz.

Gloomily, Simon greeted the men and followed Sally into the hotel.

He didn't look forward to this week-end. In one way he wanted to see Joan. He had been haunted by the memory of her even more than usual since their last meeting. He was restless by temperament, but lately he had been half-crazy with nerves and repression. His engagement was a frightful mistake. It wasn't Sally whom he wanted with all her charms and her money. Neither did he really enjoy the ceaseless pursuit of pleasure in which Sally liked to indulge, and carry him with her. There was a devil of discontent in his soul. It was Joan whom he needed. With her calm friendliness, her wisdom, her capabilities, so amazing in one of her age.

Sometimes, he gave himself up

uncontrolledly to the mad dream of holding her in his arms, of feeling those cool, clever little hands stroking his head, allowing the soothing quality of her personality to drive the devil out of him, and make him sane and whole again. He wasn't quite sane at the moment. He couldn't think straight. And now that Sally had made him fix the date of their marriage for the first of August, he felt driven beyond endurance.

He could not let her down. He did not wish to let his father down, either, nor the estate which would be ruined if he altered his plans. But there was his point of view, and feeling about Joan as he did . . .

'Simon, for heaven's sake come along. What are you dreaming about?' Sally's high, gay voice broke in on his reflections.

It was a good thing she didn't know, he thought dryly. Then, exercising his usual control, he wandered with her into the bar. It was already full of people, laughing, smoking, drinking. Sally liked this bar. She had designed it. But Simon hated it and he knew that Joan did, too. They both felt that it was a crime to put those chromium and red leather stools, and all that ostentatious, ultra-modern décor in a room which must be at least four hundred years old. A room where the massive beams were grey with age and the mullioned windows works of art. The monks had once done their writing and reading here. How their ghosts

17

must shudder, thought Simon, if they could see these people perched on the gaudy stools, tossing down one mixed drink after the other, eating potato crisps, telling racy stories, wasting time and money. But Sally liked to see it, of course. After all, it was 'business' and it all meant more profit for her.

Moodily, Simon tossed down his gin and It, and leaving Sally in conversation with an acquaintance, walked into the lounge. He liked it so much better than the bar. The huge open fireplace was unspoiled and so were the plastered walls. Old oak tables and chairs, and the cool green and white chintzes were in keeping with the spirit of the place. There were huge bowls of flowers everywhere. One particularly artistic bunch of lupins, blue lavender and pinks stood on the long refectory table in the centre of the room. He knew who had arranged those flowers. Joan.

Where was she? The hotel guests and odd arrivals were moving toward the vast dining-room which, with its tapestries and gallery, was one of the famous sights of the hotel. She might be there, having an early lunch.

Then he saw her, hurrying through a green baize door which led into the pantries. His heart leapt as he hailed her, and leapt again when he caught what he was sure was a flash of welcome for him in those beautiful eyes.

'Oh, hallo!' she greeted him.

'How are you, Joan?'

18

She was close to him now. The overall of this morning had been discarded. She might have been one of the guests. Attractive, charming in her pale grey linen dress with its yellow patterned scarf tucked into the neck, and wide yellow leather belt. He fancied that deep rose in her cheeks was for him. She was usually rather pale except for her tan, like so many dark-haired women.

'I suppose you haven't got time to come and have a drink?' he asked her.

'Gracious, no. I'm desperately busy.'

'I'm never done telling your employer how damned lucky she is to have somebody like you running this place.'

'Thank you very much.'

Joan spoke in an odd, stilted little way, but she was utterly thrilled by Simon Roxley's praise. She had had a tiring morning. It was a hot day for work. But fatigue fell away from her at the sight and sound of Simon.

It was hellish (she could only use that word), being in love with someone who belonged to someone else. Her pulses never quickened at the sight of any other man in the world. He was marvellous. So absurdly tall, he was so devastatingly attractive the grace and vitality of him, the sloe-darkness of his eyes, the slight cynicism in the twist of his well-shaped mouth. He was a bit of a cynic was Simon. A little spoiled and sure of himself. What man wouldn't be, with women rushing after him

19

the way they had rushed for Simon. Yet there was something very young and unhappy about him. That went to Joan's heart. He had by no means found the right *milieu* for him, and she knew it. Knew that Sally Vaughan could never make him happy.

'I'll see you later,' she murmured, and moved away.

He called after her:

'Let's have a talk some time?'

She wanted to answer 'yes', but dared not. What good would it do, talking to Simon? Why allow herself to be unnecessarily hurt? She made the excuse that she would be too busy. He looked after the slim figure in grey and yellow almost despairingly.

Then, shrugging his shoulders, he rejoined Sally in the bar.

Joan rarely took her meals in the restaurant while the first big rush was on. She ate her food hurriedly at a little corner table reserved for the 'management'. She had already seen Sally and been asked to lunch with her and Simon. Making the excuse of 'too much work', Joan had refused. Somehow, she did not want to be a 'third' in that particular party.

After lunch Sally sent for her.

The owner of the hotel always had the same room—the largest and most luxurious, windows looking down on to the stone terrace with its tables and gay umbrellas arranged for tea beside the river. It was one of those rooms, innumerable in England, in which Queen Elizabeth is reputed to have slept.

Sally Vaughan, in a flowered China silk wrapper, lay on the four-poster bed, conscious that the peach chintz hangings made a charming background for her fair beauty. She greeted Joan not as an employer greets one in her pay, but as her old school friend. She was always very nice to Joan and appreciative of her services.

'Quit the job and come and hear my news, honey,' she said.

Joan sat on the edge of the bed and listened to the 'news', which was exactly what she had anticipated.

For some time, Simon had been reluctant to fix a date for his wedding, because, Sally said, he did not feel he could take her and all her money unless he felt sure he was pulling his weight in a job of some kind. Now he had got that job. A firm of Insurance Brokers, anxious to have the use of his father's title, were putting Sir George on their Board and Simon in their offices. He wouldn't have to work very hard, but it would be something with a salary. They would be married in six weeks' time.

'It'll just be time for me to get my trousseau,' Sally finished, locking her hands behind her head and gazing dreamily upwards. 'Isn't that grand, Joan?'

Joan, her lashes drooping, answered:
'Grand.'

'We've decided on Budapest for our honeymoon. I've always longed for the Hungarian nights and gipsy bands and the rest of it. So has Simon.'

Joan, fingers clenched, nodded without answering but she thought:

'Simon—and a Hungarian rhapsody! Could any woman want more?'

'Then,' continued Sally, happily oblivious of the other girl's state of mind, 'we shall come back here to live, because I adore Great Friars and so does Simon. We shan't go back to London until the winter.'

Joan gave a noncommittal answer, but she was thinking:

'I shall have to resign before then. I couldn't stand it.'

'How's Ham?' Sally asked her.

'Very well.

'No relenting on your part?'

Joan stood up.

'I shall never marry a man whom I don't love, Sally.'

'You're so difficult, darling. I don't believe you'll ever fall in love.'

Joan did not reply. Aching to get out of the room, she invented a pressing appointment with one of the hotel guests and fled. Fled, before she gave herself away to the last person on earth who must ever know what sort of man she could and did love with all her heart.

CHAPTER THREE

In the early hours of that morning, Joan, who slept in a little oak-panelled room with turret-windows over the old disused chapel, was awakened first by the barking of dogs and then by a banging on her door.

'Miss Parwood! *Miss Parwood!*'

Joan switched on the light and sprang out of bed. She opened her door to a scared-looking pantry-boy who wore trousers over his pyjama suit.

'Miss, come quickly. There's a fire broke out in the staff dining-room.'

Fear clutched at Joan's heart.

The one dread of her existence was the outbreak of fire in this old place. With all its lath and plaster, it would burn like paper.

'Has somebody telephoned the Fire Brigade?'

'No, Miss. Chef and some of the others think they can get the fire out as it isn't very big.'

Joan put on a dressing gown and rushed down the corridor and back staircase after the boy. She hoped to God she could avert both a serious fire and a panic among the guests.

She found some of the male staff rushing with fire extinguishers and pails of water in and out of the staff dining-room. It was acrid with smoke and the smell of burning. She was quick to see that the outbreak was not serious. Dogs barking had wakened the pantry-boy who had smelt smoke and gone downstairs just in time. The supposition was that the trouble had been caused by one of the staff leaving a lighted cigarette near the curtains.

Joan assisted the men actively for a few moments, then stood by, issuing orders until she was certain the fire was out. Unfortunately, a stupid chambermaid had set the rumour going in the hotel. Lights were switched on, heads were thrust out of bedrooms. Nervous women, clutching their jewel cases, prepared to panic. The one person who slept through it all was the fair owner of the place who was always hard to rouse.

But Simon Roxley was up. He had had a restless night. The ashtray beside his bed was piled with cigarette ends. The lamp beside his bed had been burning when he heard the first alarm.

He caught sight of Joan, calm and poised, going from one room to another putting the guests at ease.

'The fire is right out and there is nothing whatsoever to worry about. Please go back to bed,' she kept repeating.

Gradually doors were shut and silence descended upon the hotel once more.

Dawn was breaking. White mists curled over the river and wreathed sinuously through the

24

trees. Half-awakened birds were piping. Great Friars was filled with eerie shadows, heralding the morning.

Simon Roxley walked out of his room, down the main staircase into the lounge. He found Joan standing by a lighted lamp, examining her left hand. At once he was at her side.

'I say, you haven't been hurt, have you?' She looked up quickly and put her hand behind her back.

'Heavens, how you startled me! I thought everybody had gone back to bed.'

She finished the sentence with a self-conscious little laugh, hardly daring to look at the tall, graceful figure of the man, yet swift to note how well that wine-coloured foulard dressing-gown suited him.

'Your hand,' he said. 'Did you get burnt?'

'It's nothing. I helped beat out one of the curtains which was alight . . .'

Then you have been burnt?'

He pulled her arm and insisted upon looking at the injury. At the sight of three blistered little fingers, he gave an exclamation.

'You must see to this at once. Some oil or something.'

She tried to pull her arm away.

'It's simply nothing.'

'You were grand just now,' he added, 'Getting everything under control. I watched you. For one so young, you've got extraordinary poise and grip on things.'

'Oh, it's just that I've learnt to look after myself—and others.'

'I wish you were going to look after me,' he said impulsively.

She gave another laugh, feeling ridiculously embarrassed.

'You'll soon have a wife to do that.'

He let her arm drop.

'Sally's the one who'll want looking after.'

'Can't Simon Roxley, six-foot-three, look after himself?' Joan tried to be flippant.

He looked down at her with unutterable weariness in his eyes.

'Ah! I've made a mess of things, Joan, and you know it.'

'You mustn't say that.'

'Mustn't! I'm perpetually having to say those words to myself. *Mustn't! Mustn't!* I'm sick to death of it. I *mustn't* be myself, or live my own life, or make my own choices. There's always a duty to others—others to be considered. My father, my home, my name, everything must be put before myself.' Then he broke off and added: 'Sorry! What right have I got to complain—to you of all people?'

She looked up at him, the woman in her stirred by his misery. She longed so to comfort him. She knew so well that he was chained by circumstances, that he had revolted and that he was panting to be free. That hunger for freedom—she knew so well. Didn't she, too, yearn to say and do a thousand things that she

26

must not? Things connected with him.

Simon looked down at the girl, torn with the hunger for her which had pursued him since their last meeting, when he had first realised what he felt about her. She looked very small and forlorn in the light of that single lamp. It was the first time he had seen her with her hair unbound. Curling like black silk to her shoulders. She looked like a little girl, in her rose chintz wrapper with short puffed sleeves showing her rounded, sun-browned arms. Yet he knew her to be a capable, resourceful woman. And the sight of her mouth, tender, compassionate, maddened him. In a sudden crazy moment he caught at her hand. She gave a cry of pain and at once he was filled with remorse.

'That's your blistered hand—darling—I'm so sorry!'

He had called her that name almost before he was aware of it. It had made her throat constrict. She began to tremble violently.

'I must go—back to my room.'

But all that was real and passionate and sincere in Simon Roxley had broken through the mask which he presented to the world. The devil-may-care, insouciant Simon who liked being spoiled, and whose nature warred between the spoiling and his stern sense of duty, was nothing now but a boy in love. Honestly in love for the first time in his life.

'For God's sake don't leave me, Joan,' he

27

said.

She went white, and her eyes looked, enormous and afraid.

'Simon—please . . .'

'I can't bear it, Joan. I've got to tell you. You know already. I love you. Madly, crazily. I've loved you and wanted you for weeks. I can't go through with this marriage of mine. It isn't possible, feeling as I do about you.'

She tried desperately to remain the conscientious and responsible Miss Parwood who managed this hotel. She succeeded only in being a woman, as weak and devastated by passion as Simon, himself.

She stammered:

'How do you know—what my feelings in the matter are . . .?'

His arms went round her, gathering her close. The sloe-blackness of his eyes burnt down into hers.

'Oh, I know. I'm sure that you love me. Say it. Say it, Joan, or I shall go crazy.'

'You're crazy now. And I won't say anything of the kind.'

'Little fool, I know you care. We both know it. We can neither of us go on.'

His fingers were threading through her loosened hair. Then she felt them, warm and strong, against her back. She stood there in his embrace, as she had stood a hundred times in her wild dreams. Nothing could control him now. Nothing except her denial of love. And it

28

was beyond her to make it. She leant against him, whispering brokenly:

'Simon! Simon, darling! For God's sake! We can't do this to Sally.'

'I must break with Sally and you know it.'

'You can't. I won't allow it. It's unthinkable.'

Remorselessly, he set his lips to hers. The dawn, creeping in through the mullioned windows, seemed to shatter into a thousand fragments for Joan. Her eyes closed. Blindly she returned his kiss; and during it, she felt every ounce of strength slip away from her.

At last he raised his head and said triumphantly: '*Now* is it unthinkable? *Now* can you still tell me that I must marry another woman?'

CHAPTER FOUR

It took Joan a few minutes in which to recover her balance. In Simon Roxley's arms she could not think or act sanely. He was so absolutely the lover of her imagination, the one being in the world who could make every dream of happiness which she had ever dreamed, come true.

Under the mask of efficiency, that tranquil demeanour which she presented in this hotel where she worked, Joan was just a very normal human being, a young girl in love—and badly

in love. She had never presumed that Simon
Roxley would fall in love with her. Yet he had
done so. His words, his kisses, the white-hot
fervour of his passion were not just the idle
ravings of infatuation. He loved her as she
loved him—deeply and sincerely. He never
had loved Sally. And that made it all the
harder for Joan. To be aware of that fact, and
to have to fight it, and fight herself.

Just for an instant, she clung to him, lifting
her eager mouth to his, blindly drinking in the
sweetness of his embrace; knowing that such
an embrace must mean either heaven or hell
for any woman. And this was heaven, only
it was not lasting. She knew, even while she
savoured its rapture, that an utter purgatory
lay beyond. For it was a heaven to which
neither of them had any right. And which both
of them must forgo.

Using every vestige of her will-power, she
drew away from him. Her scorched fingers
were hurting violently, but the physical
discomfort was secondary to the mental
conflict of this thing.

She said:

'No, Simon. No more. You mustn't kiss me
again—please!'

'Why?'

'You know why.'

He laughed a little under his breath and
shook his head. She looked up at him dumbly.
He was so unlike the Simon whom she knew;

the lazy, cynical young man with his half-weary air of indifference to the world; an indifference which she knew sprang from a dozen difficulties and cross-purposes within him. The attractive, handsome boy had been spoiled from his birth and yet cheated. Life had cheated him. Perhaps he had cheated himself too. But somehow he had missed the way and had found neither true happiness nor peace of mind. His distaste and secret rebellion lay in the sombre darkness of those eyes under the half-drooping lids, and in the slightly ironic twist of his lips. But not now. Now he was transformed. Passionately eager and glowing with the warmth of a fire which she knew must be genuine. Whatever else had passed Simon Roxley by, love had touched him. Real love for her, Joan Parwood. And that knowledge both amazed and devastated her. To resist was to be scarcely human. Yet to surrender would be inhuman cruelty to that other woman to whom he was engaged.

Said Simon:

'I see no earthly reason why I should not kiss you again, again and again, my sweet. I love you. Do you hear that? I love you madly, hopelessly, and for ever.'

'You can't, Simon. You mustn't.'

'You're wrong, Joan. Tell a man not to speak or move and he can do as you ask. But you can not tell him not to love. That's out of his power. It is out of my power to stop loving

31

you.'

She pushed back the dark veil of her hair which had drifted across her eyes. Her face, her throat were burning. In the dim light of the solitary lamp, her large, hazel eyes were bright as stars. He thought she was the loveliest thing he had ever looked upon. Little, lovely and sweet, with her black, tumbled hair, her sun-browned arms, small and slim and provocative . . . he felt intoxicated with love for her. He had thought himself in love many times in his life. But nothing like this had ever happened to him and he knew that all the other loves had been as false as they were fugitive.

'I fell in love with you when we danced together last time I was down here, Joan,' he said. 'You know that, don't you?'

'Yes. But . . .'

'And you love me too, don't you?'

'I won't tell you.'

'Darling little idiot! You've already told me that by the way you kissed me just now.'

'I was mad.'

'We may both be mad, but we do love each other. If you can deny that, Joan, you'll deny the greatest truth life has to offer.'

'Simon, there's Sally.'

The eager, boyish light sped suddenly from his eyes.

'I know. That's the devil.'

That's what makes it impossible—for us.'

'How practical you are. And I've always

been such a crazy being, Joan. Always needed somebody like you to help me be cool and cautious and logical.'

'Please don't sneer at me.'

'Good God! I don't mean to sneer. You know I find you absolutely wonderful—but . . .'

'But we have *got* to remember Sally.'

'Yes,' he said morosely. 'I suppose we have.'

'You must forget about this. So must I.'

'Quite impossible. And you know it.'

'Well, we can't let Sally down.'

'I'm afraid your loyalty exceeds mine, my dear.'

'But Simon, you're going to marry her!'

He folded his arms and looked down at her, his dark, narrow eyes tired and ironic again.

'You're quite shocked at my disloyalty, aren't you?'

'No, it isn't that,' she said lamely.

'Yes. You think, rightly and properly, Joan, that I should not have told you that I love you. Well, I think I was also right to do so. I've had to be insincere all my life. Always doing what was expected of me, never what I wanted. But I've wanted this, and I've done it. I've told you that I care for you more than I have cared for any woman in my life. I've got to be sincere about you, if about nobody and nothing else.'

Every word he said went straight down to her heart and was imprinted indelibly on her memory. She loved him so much. But

33

she tried to fight on, desperately; to act as she considered right, in the face of her own principles. It was all she could do to stop from throwing herself into his arms and asking him to keep her there and never let her go. She had to remind herself again and again that Sally existed, that he was going to marry her. She had to keep repeating to herself the old, hackneyed words: *'I could not love thee dear so much, loved I not honour more.'* Honour stood in the way of this love, Simon's honour, and hers. Their honour toward a woman who had been good to them both.

Simon was speaking, cutting through the confusion of her thoughts:

'Do you blame me for telling you that I love you?'

Mutely she shook her head.

'And do you admit that you love me, too?'

She battled frantically with all the warm impulses in her nature.

'Simon, you're not being fair.'

He caught her arms and drew her close to him again.

'You've got to answer me that. Do you love me, Joan, do you?'

'If I do, what good can it be to either of us?' she said wildly.

'God! I don't know. I only know that we were meant for each other, darling.'

That was wrung from his heart. A passionate, genuine cry that found an echo in her own soul. Weak and trembling, she lay against his breast and found herself caught up in the feverish ecstasy of another long embrace. And again she returned his kiss. Her arms were tight locked about his neck. Words she had never meant to utter tumbled, white-hot, from her lips.

'I adore you—worship you! Darling, darling Simon . . . You don't know how much I love you. Simon, kiss me again . . . again!'

Then, when the tidal wave of their mutual passion, drowning and drenching all else, receded and flung them high and dry onto the shore of hard, cold reality again, they found themselves sitting side by side on a sofa in that deserted lounge, talking, arguing, finally admitting the impossibility of the whole affair.

'You couldn't let Sally down,' Joan kept saying. 'We neither of us could face her in the morning and tell her what we feel. You agree with that, don't you, Simon?'

He sat back in his own corner, lit a cigarette and strove to regain his control. She could see his hand shaking as it carried the cigarette to his lips. Such fine, sensitive hands were Simon's. She had always admired them. And the touch of them filled her with a delight that was almost anguish. But that was what, in future, she must try to forget. The rapture of being touched, kissed, loved by Simon.

'I suppose you're right,' at length he said, as though the words had been dragged from him by force.

She gave a long sigh. She, too, sat back in her corner and nursed her blistered fingers, becoming more conscious every moment of physical pain. And never in her life before had she known what it was to feel so tired.

Many a time after a rush in the hotel she had felt worn out. But this was fatigue of another kind. It was as though she had been battered and bruised by a storm. She felt unfit to cope with Simon or herself. It had been a tussle from the moment his arms had closed around her. She had wanted so much to give in. It had rested with her, as it always must rest with the woman, to make the final decision. Well, she had made it, forbidden him to tell Sally the truth. For that was what he had wanted to do. To go frankly and openly to Sally and confess that he could not marry her because he was in love with someone else.

But Joan had told him that could never be. First of all because he had given Sally his word, and Sally was her friend to whom she owed much. Therefore, they both owed it to her to keep faith and resist this new-found love of theirs. And secondly, because there were still grave reasons why he must marry a girl with means. Someone who could help restore the tottering fortunes of the Roxleys. It would be madness, she had protested, from every point of view, if he broke his engagement with Sally Vaughan and married Joan Parwood.

36

'I suppose you are right, Joan,' he said again, 'but it's the most damnable thing that's ever happened.'

'It's happened often, Simon. We're not the first pair to find out that we love each other and have to say "good-bye".'

He turned and looked at her. The cigarette smoke cleared away. He saw her face, very pale, pinched with fatigue. Her eyes looked enormous and immeasurably sad.

'Oh, darling,' he said, 'how on earth am I going to say good-bye to you?'

We've both got to face it, Simon. It's no easier for me.'

'You seem so much braver than I am.'

'You don't know what a coward I feel inside.'

'Well, you don't show it. I suppose I'm a cad, even for this night's disloyalty to Sally. And God knows, it hasn't gone very far.'

'Far enough, Simon. Or am I a prig? I don't want to be one. I don't *feel* like one.'

'You're not one, sweet. You're just frightfully decent about Sally. I want to be decent about her, too. But I'm not quite sane. You've gone utterly and completely to my head, and heaven knows how I'm going to get you out of it.'

'We've both got to make the effort, haven't we?'

'If you really believe that it's doing the right thing.'

'Don't you?'

He stubbed the end of his cigarette in an ashtray.

'I'm not so sure. Can it be right for me to marry Sally, even to save my family, knowing that I love you?'

'Yes. Because it isn't only for you to say. You cared about Sally once.'

'I'm still fond of her. But it isn't comparable with what I feel about you.

'Still, you have agreed that we can't let her down?' He moved his head from side to side as though driven beyond endurance.

'Oh, yes! But I wish to God one had no sense of honour. No conscience. And that you weren't so frightfully logical and fair and all the rest of it!'

She felt infinitely tender toward him. He was so like a young spoiled boy. She loved him so much. It would have been marvellous if they could both have taken what they wanted out of life, regardless of anyone else. But that wasn't possible. And she dared not let him know how equally she resented fate having done this to them. How equally she resented having to fight her love. Indeed, it would not take much to break down her own defences.

'Darling, we must make a show of it, anyhow. Mustn't we?' she said.

'Yes. I'll do my best.'

'Sally does love you, Simon.'

He frowned and nodded.

Joan was right in a way. Sally was devoted in her fashion. But he did not think Sally's way of loving a man could be put on a parallel with Joan's. Joan would love deeply and devotedly for love's sake. There was an indomitable streak in her. A determination in this young, beautiful girl which drew both amazement and respect from him. Whatever she did she would do well and to the best of her ability. But Sally was much more on the surface. She did not take life seriously. She was flippant, spoiled and self-centred. Their marriage might be amusing and a mutual benefit. But it could never be a true marriage, a real, serious union of mind, body and soul, such as he had always wanted his marriage to be. Still, Sally would definitely suffer if he jilted her now. He could not but agree with Joan about that.

'We must make a show of it,' Joan repeated.

And he answered:

'I'll do my best. But if it gets too much—I'll just have to tell you, that's all.'

She felt a pain in her heart that was increasing every instant. The pain of realising that she must never belong to him. And she faced the even greater pain of seeing him marry someone else. She was almost frightened by the thought that he might not be able to go through with it. If he weakened in his resolve to marry Sally, what could she, Joan, do? How could she continue to resist the greatest living force within herself . . . her utter love for him?

She said quickly:

'We mustn't even think like that, Simon. We must try to behave tomorrow as though nothing has happened. And, of course, once you and Sally are married, I shall resign from this post. I couldn't stay here.' He felt so wretched about the whole affair that he did not even protest against that. He said heavily:

'We could have made something so marvellous out of life together, Joan.'

She leaned back her head and shut her eyes in an exhausted way.

'Yes.'

'We both like the same things. Do you remember that talk we had about country life? How we both love horses and dogs. You told, me you used to ride when you were a little girl, and there's nothing I love more than being on the back of a horse. But it bores Sally. It's racing cars she's crazy about.'

'It was like that at school,' said Joan dreamily. 'I was always crazy about riding. I wanted to save up and buy a horse. But Sally wanted a car. While my father was alive, we lived in Sussex. But when he died, my mother and I had to live in a small flat. I just hated it.'

'Then you started work?'

'Yes.

'It seems all wrong that you should have had to earn your living. I would like to have given you so much. I would like to have taken you to

40

Roxley Hall—my home. That's in the Sussex you love. There are always horses to ride and dogs to walk with you, down there. You would have fitted in so well. But Sally hates the quiet of it. That's why she wants to live in her hotel. She must have noise and people and parties.'

'Poor Simon!'

'Oh, don't pity me,' he said in a savage tone. 'I'm too disgustingly full of self-pity as it is. I'll make the best of it, as you want me to.'

She said forlornly:

'If I had what I wanted, Simon, it would be only you. Nobody else in the world.'

'My sweet! My sweet Joan . . .'

He turned to her swiftly, burying his hot lips in the palm of her hand. Then, when he felt her wince, he remembered her injuries. He stood up and lifted her onto her feet.

'Darling! What a brute I've been, forgetting your poor little hand. You must have it dressed straight away.'

'It's nothing. I'll go up and see to it now.'

They both looked about them in a dazed way, half-astonished to see that the lounge was filled with morning light and that it was long past daybreak. Outside the windows, the birds were chirruping an ecstatic chorus.

With a sinking heart, Joan realised that a fresh day had begun. It would be a glorious June morning and one big rush in the hotel. She would have a thousand things to do and no time even to think of Simon and all that she must bottle up. She met his gaze, and he held out his arms.

'Will you say good-bye?'

She trembled violently, but shook her head.

'Not like that! I couldn't . . . I can't bear any more, Simon. Oh Simon, darling! . . .' Her voice broke.

She felt courage, honour, everything but her love, for him slipping away from her. Panic-stricken, she fled from the lounge and left him standing there.

Fled up to her own room. Shut and locked her door, then lay, face-downwards on her bed, feeling that her very heart had broken.

CHAPTER FIVE

It was a 'black' Sunday for Joan. How she got through the long, arduous day's work she did not know. The warm June weather brought crowds for lunch, tea and supper to Great Friars. Already the hotel was packed. On such occasions the staff was over-worked, and it was Joan who lent a hand here and there when she could, and where she was wanted. She might have sat in her office, putting the various jobs on the shoulders of subordinates. But it was not in her nature to do that. She could never sit down and watch the staff severely taxed. She was here, there, everywhere, until she was so tired that she could scarcely stand; so hot, that it was as though she were feverish, and her head was splitting with pain.

It was Miss Parwood wanted in the kitchens to settle a dispute. Miss Parwood, to speak to the gardener, who wouldn't bring in enough flowers for the extra tables. Miss Parwood, to lock and unlock the linen cupboard a dozen times. Fresh linen here, new stores from the still-room, more catering wanted, difficult guests to placate, cars to be ordered. (The latter she could put safely into the hands of Ham, who was always to be relied upon.) Special trays to be sent up to somebody who was ill. Miss Parwood always saw to such trays herself. It was because of her conscientious supervision that Great Friars ran so smoothly and so well and had the name of being the perfect hotel.

But the consequence was, that Miss Parwood herself suffered from nerves and exhaustion when such days came to an end. And on this Sunday, glad though she was to have the work to take her mind off Simon, her task had never seemed more uncongenial.

She longed to get away from the noise and the people, the chatter, the demands; to steal out into those lovely gardens, down to the river's edge, into a punt; to let herself drift on the cool water and find a spot where the willows and the alders cast a green shade and she could be alone. Alone with her dreams and her thoughts of *him.*

How impossible to forget the dawn and those moments in his arms. Moments fraught with the highest rapture and the deepest pain. She had been so determined with him. But for herself, now that it was over, she needed determination. It was sheer agony to know that he was there in the hotel with Sally, yet not dare to approach him. To catch glimpses of them every now and then. The tall, graceful man in white flannels, playing tennis with the beautiful fair-haired girl whom he was to marry; or sitting under a striped umbrella in the gardens, drinking tea with her. Or later, in the bar, getting through one cocktail after another. Oh yes, she saw enough of that to realise that he was drinking more cocktails than usual, trying, like herself, to forget. To hear him laugh and exchange a flippant word with Sally or one of their friends. He was putting a mask on for the world. Underneath that mask, he was suffering. That she knew. She had not the slightest doubt of the genuineness of the love which he had revealed to her in the early hours of this morning.

They had not spoken to each other since then. But once or twice he had come near enough to look at her. Each time, it had been a long, poignant exchange of hopeless love and longing from his gaze to hers. Enough to make her pulse-beats quicken deliriously. Then, when he had passed on, those beats died down to a slow, aching throb. It was all so useless. It would have been so much better had they never come together in that lounge after the fire and admitted what they felt about each other.

One thing which comforted her was that Sally did not guess. She had had to see Sally about claiming the insurance for the fire and putting the staff-room back into order. Sally, as usual, bored with the business side of the hotel, had told her to do what she wanted and use her own discretion. And, as usual, she had been charming.

'You're looking as white as a ghost, my dear,' she had said. 'For heaven's sake don't work yourself to death. Let the others get on with it.'

Joan had smiled and assured her that she was not doing too much, and that her pallor was due to the unusual heat.

But after she had left Sally, she had a few moments of bitter conflict within herself. She was fond of the girl who had been so kind to her and given her this marvellous job. She admired her dazzling good looks, her wit and humour. The last thing she wished to do was to feel antipathy towards Sally. But she could not resist a very human jealousy—an almost passionate envy of her, now. To have the luck to marry Simon! Did Sally know how lucky she was? And could she possibly make him the sort of wife he deserved? No, it didn't seem possible that Sally could be right for Simon. The Simon who had held her hand and spoken with contempt and dislike of his useless existence, and revealed to her his dreams of country life and of doing something worthwhile. Poor Simon! Darling, devilishly attractive Simon, whose touch, whose kiss, could lift a woman to the stars—a woman who loved him as much as she did!

Coals of fire were heaped upon Joan's head when Sally sent her waiter to her office with a request that she should join her and Simon for dinner that night. There was always dancing in the big hall in the summer evenings.

'Madame would like you to dine and dance, Miss,' the waiter told the young manageress with the courtesy which all the staff showed Joan. It was agreed by most of them that she was a just and considerate young lady to work for, and her personality was such that none of the servants took advantage of her youth.

Joan, for an instant, savoured the thought of dining and dancing with Simon, then dismissed it from her mind. She could not possibly stand it. Besides, she felt too unutterably weary. She wanted to go to her room and be alone.

She wrote a swift note to Sally, thanking her but pleading fatigue. This she sent up to Miss Vaughan's suite. She then settled down to her desk to attend to a query on a big bill which the cashier had just handed her.

She was quite unprepared for a visit from

Simon himself. He walked into the office without knocking, startling her. She looked up at him, pen poised in her hand, cheeks flooding with hot colour. Already he was in white tie and tails. He looked marvellous like that, she thought, with almost personal pride in his tall, slim figure. There was a white carnation in his buttonhole which gave him a festive look. But there was nothing festive about his expression. His sloe-black eyes were gloomy, brooding.

'Forgive the interruption,' he said stiffly. 'I was sent by Sally. She insisted that I should persuade you to join us this evening.

Joan laid down her pen. She answered as stiffly: 'It's very kind of Sally, and of you, to ask me. But I'd rather not, thank you.'

'Is it really because you're tired?'

'Yes.'

He looked at her intently. A golden glow from the lamp on her desk gave her a spurious colour. But he could see the black lines of fatigue carved under her eyes, and the weary droop of her slender shoulders. It infuriated him to think that she was so hard-worked, such a slave to this hotel. Sally's slave! And upstairs, he had just left his fiancée having her nails manicured, raving about the new evening dress which she was going to wear, fit and glowing after two hours' rest and massage from her personal maid. Luxury, ease, all that she wanted. Spoiled and self centred. Epithets that he sometimes applied to himself. But Joan had no time in which to think of herself. Joan regarded life as a battlefield rather than a playground. And God! What a gallant fight she made! He was filled with an intolerable longing to do something for her; maddened by his inability to do anything at all.

He shut the office door behind him, came forward and leant over the desk.

'I damn well refuse to spend this evening amusing Sally, while you work yourself to death,' he said roughly.

'I shan't be doing that. I shall go to bed.'

'It's because of me that you aren't joining the party, isn't it?'

'Partly that,' she admitted.

'Perhaps you are right. Perhaps it wouldn't be a very good trio.'

'Obviously not.'

He suddenly beat a fist on the desk.

'I can't stand it. It's so hideously unfair. I've been at Sally's beck and call all day, and now . . .'

'Simon,' Joan interrupted, 'you forget that your place is with Sally.'

'Oh, yes. You can remind me of that. And I dare-say it's my place to gallivant with her for the rest of time. But . . .'

'Simon,' she interrupted again, 'don't, my dear. We've been over all that. We decided, didn't we, that you couldn't let her down?'

'Why always "her"—"her"? Why not

consider yourself, myself, for a change?'

Joan stood up and turning her back on Simon, seized her bag and drew out a packet of cigarettes. Her nerves were jumping so, she needed a smoke, although she never allowed herself to do so when on duty in the hotel.

'We mustn't think this way, Simon,' she said in a low tone. 'It can't do any good and you've promised. Oh! You belong to Sally and you know it.'

'The Simon who belongs to Sally is the man who has never taken life seriously until now, and who was glad to give his fine old name and future title in exchange for an attractive, moneyed wife. But the real Simon belongs to you, Joan, only to you.'

She did not look at him. But he saw her shaking as she lit a cigarette. He came and caught at her wrist.

'Are you flesh and blood, Joan, or just a machine? A machine that works for the cause of right and honour and principle, but is deaf to the call of love.'

Then she turned on him, cheeks flaming, eyes ablaze.

'You know that isn't true! You know it wasn't a machine you held in your arms this morning.'

His whole face lit up and he became young and eager again.

'Ah, darling. I do know. You were sweet. And you do love me still?'

'You know it. But go away, Simon, and leave me alone, for God's sake.'

His hand dropped away from her.

'Sorry. I forgot myself.'

She gave an hysterical little laugh.

'I can forget myself quite easily, too. There's nothing I want to do more. But unfortunately, neither of us must forget Sally.'

'You're right, and I'm wrong again.'

'Don't you love Sally any more at all?' she asked almost piteously.

'I'm terribly fond of her, Joan. One can't help that. She's so good-natured and generous. But feeling as I do about you, it drives me crazy to even contemplate marriage with her or any other woman.'

'But the date for the wedding is fixed, Simon.'

He put a hand up to his eyes.

'Yes.'

'It's hell for both of us,' she said. 'And the sooner I leave this place, the better. But it can't be until Sally comes back. I couldn't let a stranger manage the hotel while she's away on her honeymoon.'

'Oh, damn that word!'

'I don't enjoy using it—or thinking about it, I assure you.'

The office door opened. Into the room came Sally Vaughan, white and shining in a new décolletée dress which was embroidered with silver, a camellia in her fair curls, diamonds sparkling on her neck and in her ears. She was heavily made-up. Much more so than need be. Her eye-lashes looked an incredible length. She had a gay greeting for her fiancé and her friend.

'Hi, you two! Simon, I want a drink. Joanie, run up and get on your tiara, darling, and let's have a gay evening.'

Joan managed a smile.

'It's awfully sweet of you, Sally. Simon's been trying to persuade me. But I really am too tired. No, it's not work—don't think that. Just a bad head.'

Sally put an arm through Simon's and hung on to it affectionately.

'Isn't she a bad girl, honey? I don't believe its a headache at all. I think she's just being tactful about the "young couple"! But we'd like to have her with us, wouldn't we?'

Simon stiffened and looked away from Joan. 'Of course.'

'Well, join us later if you feel like it, ducky,' said Sally.

'Thank you,' said Joan, wishing that she did not feel so guilty and that Sally would not always be so kind. It was so ghastly to be in love with the lover of one's friend and employer. And she could see, from Simon's expression, what he was feeling. Yet she could not help remembering what he had said just now. Why must they always think of Sally, he had argued, why not of themselves.

Then she thrust that dangerous thought away from her.

'I must go up and change,' she said desperately.

But even with her back turned to him, she could feel Simon's dark, brooding gaze following her.

As she opened her office-door, a man's tall, broad figure barred her exit. Ham, still in grey flannels and an open shirt. He gave her his school-boy's grin and nodded to Simon and Sally.

'Good-evening.'

The greeting was returned. Then Ham's blue eyes sped to Joan.

'Just coming to see if you'd like a spin after office hours. Got a new sports Bentley to try out. Boy! What a chassis!'

Silence. The cheerful voice found no echo in Joan's heart, and Simon glared. He knew and liked William Hamley. But did the young man make a habit of coming here and taking Joan out 'after office hours'? Jealousy tore at him. A jealousy he had no right to feel.

He was not even allowed to hear Joan's answer. Sally dragged him away, protesting that she had waited long enough for her *apéritif.*

In the bar, Simon was so preoccupied that even Sally's bright stream of artificial chatter wavered. Glass poised in hand, she pouted at him with lips roughed to a bright vermilion.

'*Aren't* you the play-boy of Britain!' she said with playful sarcasm.

He gave her a steely smile.

'It isn't exactly a status for which I am qualifying!'

'Why, honey,' Sally said, wide-eyed, 'I wasn't being serious. What's bitten you?'

He saw the corners of her lips go down like a hurt child's. He strove desperately to get on top of his conflicting emotions. What right had he to be irritable with Sally? It wasn't her fault that he had fallen in love with her friend. Neither was there any use in wondering whether that healthy, grinning young man from the garage had induced Joan to go out in his new car. Joan had begged him to 'make a show of it.' That's what she was doing. So he must do the same. But supposing she turned to Hamley for comfort? God! What a thought to knock the bottom out of a man's world. When he wanted with every vestige of his being to take her into his arms and keep her there.

With a great effort he put out a hand and laid it on Sally's knee.

'Sorry, darling. Got a liver. We'll dance it off after dinner.'

Sally smiled again. Nothing went very deep with her. Neither her loves nor her hates. She coveted the thrill of the moment. And at the moment, the big thrill was Simon and her coming marriage. It would be fun to marry him and later to become Lady Roxley. Old Sir

George wouldn't last long. Eventually Roxley Hall would be theirs, a lovely, historic, 'spooky' place where she could give heavenly parties.

Of course she knew quite well that her money was needed to put the old place on its feet again and keep up the immense property. Also, it would help keep Simon in the Society 'swim', from which he would soon have to exclude himself unless his finances looked up. He was awfully fond of his family and name. He had a young brother, Vivian, at Sandhurst. Vivian had always wanted to go into the Guards. And he couldn't afford that unless there was money behind him. Sally liked to be a philanthropist when her heart was touched. She was in love with Simon, and young Vivian, who had Simon's charm if not his looks, amused her. As soon as she was Mrs. Simon Roxley, she would see that Vivian got into his crack regiment.

So far as she knew, Simon was as pleased as she was with the match they were going to make. It never entered her head that he would look seriously at any other girl. He was nice to all pretty women. Joan Parwood was a beautiful girl and no doubt he gave her an occasional look out of the corners of his handsome eyes. But what did that matter? Sally, even in the midst of her engagement, never took it amiss if an attractive man made a 'slight pass' at her. She accepted Simon's excuse about his 'liver attack' in perfect faith, smiled again, and prepared to enjoy her evening mightily.

CHAPTER SIX

Joan did not take that drive with Ham. She told him what she had told the others—that she was dead tired. But she did not go to bed. She was too tired for sleep. She was in need of fresh air—and solitude.

An hour or so after dinner, she left the hotel and its crowds behind her and walked into the grounds of Great Friars. Every window blazed with light. From the dance-band, which played every night in the big hall, came the haunting melody of a Viennese waltz. The June night was cool and crisp. There was a full moon that carved strange shadows out of the trees and flung them into grotesque silhouettes upon the smooth lawns.

Down by the river, away from the terrace where the hotel guests sat or wandered, Joan found a favourite place of her own where she could hide from her work and from those who worked with her.

At the far end of the old, disused cloisters, there was a wooden bench under an old pear tree. And close to the bench, a stone pedestal bearing the grey stone figure of a nymph. A statue which had probably been put there by a

Tudor lord of this manor, to replace a Saint's shrine, after the monks had been turned out of Great Friars during the Reformation.

The nymph was poised for flight, stone fingers clasped against her breast in an attitude of supplication, head turned, looking over her shoulder as though at someone who pursued. Often Joan had woven fanciful stories around the nymph. Into the stone eyes she read terror and despair. From whom was she fleeing? An evil, mischievous faun, or a shepherd boy, her own lover? Perhaps the latter. That was what Joan imagined tonight. The poor nymph was flying from love, just as she, herself, must fly from it. And she wished to God she could change places with that statue and be cold and unfeeling and passionless, the tears frozen for ever on her lashes. It was so hard to be alive, warm and aching for a love which could never be hers.

Joan put an arm on the back of the bench and leant her head against it.

'Simon, Simon,' she whispered his name.

From the distance she could hear the faint echo of the dance-band. But above it rose the piercing sweet treble of a nightingale, the first she had heard this summer. Joan raised her head and sighed. The bird's song was lovely. But that, too, was a message of love. Love, love was everywhere. And the air was perfumed with the scent of wild thyme and syringa, and with the jasmine that clustered in starry blossoms around the pedestal of the statue. One of the most romantic places in the world was Great Friars. Quite the wrong spot for her at the moment, she thought drearily. The one thing she wanted to do was to get away from romance. But nothing, nothing could erase the thought of Simon. Simon, dancing in there with Sally. Lucky Sally, who in six weeks' time would be his wife.

The hand which had been burned during the fire outbreak early this morning was bandaged now and throbbed painfully. Even that reminded Joan of Simon, who had kissed every finger. How she loved him! How hard she tried to resist him when they were face to face, and yet, at an hour like this, when she was alone, she felt that not even her loyalty to Sally could prevent her from going to him if he asked her a second time.

She sat there until she grew cold in spite of the camel's-hair coat which she had put over her blue chiffon dinner-dress.

What use to sit here and brood about Simon? Just one more cigarette and she would turn in to bed. But before she could strike the match, she heard footsteps. In between two bushes she saw the red point of a cigar, and knew that her retreat had been discovered. She saw nothing for a second but that tiny red glow, because this place was so thickly surrounded by trees that even the moonlight was excluded.

'Who is it?' she asked sharply.

Then the one voice which she most wanted to hear, yet dreaded hearing, answered:

'Good Lord! Is that you, Joan?'

She sprang up, then stood still. Unconsciously, her hands flew to her breast. She was the nymph come to life, ready for flight; pitilessly pursued by her lover. No escape was possible. Simon stepped into the enchanted circle and was there before her, looking down at her with a look which told her that he, too, was haunted by their love. She could faintly discern the wildness in those sloe-black eyes of his. His voice, when he spoke again, was wild.

'Oh Joan, thank God I've found you. I can't go on like this. Darling, I can't!'

She shivered and shook her head at him.

'What is it, Simon?'

He threw his cigar away and caught her hands.

'I've been crazy for you all day, Joan. Ever since this morning. It drove me mad seeing you in the office this evening. Seeing you with that man. He's in love with you. I tell you I can't stand it!'

'But my dear, I'm not in love with him. Ham's only my friend.'

That doesn't matter. He has a right to make love to you. Every man has except myself.'

'No one, *no one* will ever be allowed to make love to me but you.'

'And not me! You forbid me. And I try to forbid myself. But I don't think I'm as strong-minded as you are.

He was crushing her fingers against his breast. He seemed forgetful of her bandaged hand, and she scarcely noticed the physical pain. She only knew that her heart was beating madly and that there was joy within her now. The joy of being close to him, alone with him once again. It was a delirious feeling over which she had little control. Her feeling for him was too vital and too compelling to be annihilated by any reminder of principles or loyalties. He was not married to Sally. There was still time for him to get out of that marriage, and be free to become hers—all hers. That was what he was saying now, the words tumbling hotly and recklessly from his lips.

'I couldn't go through with it, Joan. You couldn't let me. Listen! This has only been one day—and it's been like a whole year of frightfulness. Trying not to let Sally see what I feel, or give way to my love for you. If every day in the future is to be like this one, it would drive me out of my mind . . .' he gave a short laugh . . . 'What would be the good of a lunatic husband to poor Sally?'

Joan thrilled to those words. How could she do otherwise than experience fierce pride and satisfaction in the knowledge that she could make Simon Roxley feel so about her?

She hadn't meant to. The whole thing had just happened before either of them realised it. This love had come upon them unawares, and it was too strong. It was beating down the poor little defences they had put up for Sally's sake.

'I've had plenty of time to think things over, Joan,' went on Simon, 'and I don't feel this would be fair to Sally. Our honeymoon would be a farce. Every time I kiss her now, I feel dead. She'll soon wake up to that. It just wouldn't be fair, I tell you. And that's not only thinking of you and me, but of her.'

Joan felt that she was sinking, drowning. Very soon she would not be able to keep her head up above water. She, too, had been trying all day and had found the effort appalling. She, too, had begun to wonder if it would be fair to Sally if Simon married her without telling her what he felt. Yet she tried to protest.

'Don't you think it will get better, Simon? Wouldn't it be easier if we didn't see each other? This week-end hasn't been a fair trial. Tomorrow you'll be going up to town to work. You won't see me. You'll only see Sally.'

'If I left you and went to the other side of the world, I would still see no woman except you,' he said.

'Oh Simon, then what can we do?'

He made no answer, but took her into his arms. For an instant he saw the lovely warmth and sweetness in her eyes. Then his lips were against hers. Like two people dying of thirst they exchanged those long, deep kisses. The stone girl stood blind and motionless on her pedestal beside the passionate lovers. And the nightingale went on singing jubilantly. Joan felt that she was lost. That Simon was lost. And poor Sally, she too was lost, in a different way.

It was only the remembrance of Sally that brought Joan down from the stars. She felt indeed that, with the stars and moon, she had been whirling in space, locked in the arms of this man who had the power to move her so poignantly. There could never be another Simon. He, and he alone, could make life for her—or mar it.

He murmured endearments, caressing her hair and her cheeks, kissing her throat, telling her a dozen times how much he needed her.

'You're so sweet, Joan. Darling, there could never be anybody, but you. It's out of the question for me to think of marrying Sally now.'

She stood, with her eyes hidden against his shoulder, one hand against his smooth, dark head.

'Simon, we're frightful cads! How can we tell her?'

'You don't think after these few moments tonight that I could marry her, do you?'

'Naturally I don't want to think so.'

'Well, if it's a question of honour, Joan, it wouldn't be honourable to marry her without telling her.'

'I suppose not. But I still don't think we've given it a fair chance.'

'Sweet, you know as well as I do, that if we waited a year or two years, we'd feel just the same about each other.'

'If we didn't see each other we might gather enough courage to accept the situation.'

'But, darling,' he argued, 'why accept a situation which is false? It couldn't be anything but false for me to make Sally my wife when I am crazily in love with you.'

She hung back in his arms.

'But there are so many other issues.'

He moved his head impatiently.

'My family—Roxley Hall—I know all that.'

'Well?' she asked lamely.

'Well, why the hell should I sacrifice myself and you to them? I'm prepared to work my fingers to the bone to keep you. I know you wouldn't mind living in a quiet way with me. Roxley Hall must go. My father must accept it. And my brother—well, why should he be put into a regiment for the idle rich, and be bolstered up? He must make his own way, too.'

'Are you quite sure you want that?'

'I know it wouldn't be right to marry Sally now,' he said stubbornly. 'She'll be the first to say so.'

Joan drew out of his arms gently. She sat down on the bench, because her knees were trembling so.

'Oh, Simon, I can't bear the thought of telling poor Sally. She may be flippant and superficial. I know she is in a way, but I think she cares for you, my dear, and it will be an awful shock to her. To her pride, if nothing else.'

He looked down at her with unutterable tenderness in his eyes.

'You're a grand girl, Joan. You put yourself last every time.'

'I have no right to take away another woman's future husband, Simon.'

'You won't be taking me away, darling. I'm insisting upon taking you.'

Joan thrust her hands into her coat-pockets. The palms were moist. Her disordered hair clung damply to her forehead. Her cheeks, her lips, were still burning from his kisses. But there was a cold, fearful little feeling in her heart.

'Simon, I almost agree with you. I'm almost past fighting and ready to admit that it would be wrong of you to marry Sally now. But I still feel that we ought to give it one more chance.'

'Darling, the marriage is fixed for the first of August. The longer we leave it, the worse it will be for her.'

'You might regret it, Simon. I don't even know why you love me. I've nothing on earth to offer you.

'And what have I to offer you, my sweet? An empty title in the future. A dwindling income and a faint possibility of making my living in the City. But you've got every quality a man could wish for in a wife. Besides which, I just love you, and that's that.'

'I adore you, Simon,' she said. 'But let's not do anything in a mad hurry. Let's give it just one week of thought. It's only fair to her.'

'Are you afraid you might be making a mistake about me?' he asked tensely.

'No.'

'Then are you afraid that *I* am just infatuated with you for the moment?'

'No,' she repeated, biting her lip. 'But it's taking a terrific and irrevocable step if you marry me instead of Sally. And it's affecting so many other people's lives, that it does want very careful thought. Don't you agree?'

An instant's hesitation, then he made a gesture of hopelessness.

'I don't know,' he said between his teeth; 'you're so frighteningly strong-minded, Joan.'

There came a woman's high, gay voice, cutting through the stilly night:

'Si—mon! Oh, Si—mon!'

Joan stood up.

'That's Sally.'

Simon caught Joan into his arms in another desperate embrace.

'Darling, darling Joan, let's tell her now? Let's face the inevitable and tell her what we feel? It'll be kinder to her and to ourselves not to prolong the agony.'

CHAPTER SEVEN

It cost Joan the greatest effort of her life to refuse Simon that request. It was more than an ordinary one. It was a wild plea for his happiness and hers. That he was serious she could have no doubt. He wanted her, Joan, for his wife instead of Sally. And realising how much he would benefit by a union with Sally, Joan could not restrain the surge of pride, of sheer feminine vanity which thrilled through her very being at that knowledge.

But resist she must. She could not hear Sally calling Simon in that gay carefree way, then face her and explode a bomb at her feet which would shatter her little world. It might be a frivolous world, a world which for her was centred in the most shallow pleasures, but it *was*—Sally's world.

Joan pushed Simon away from her.

'No, no, no, not now!' she gasped. 'We can't do it, Simon.'

'I tell you we must.'

'Not now. Not tonight.'

'Then it only means delaying it for another day.'

'But Simon . . .'

'It's no good, Joan,' he interrupted, 'I can't go on with Sally. She must know the truth.'

An agony of loyalty toward her school friend

and benefactor tore Joan, just as Simon's love for her and her love for him was tearing her.

'Give it one more week. I agree with you that it can't go on like this, but let us go away from each other just for this week and come to a final decision next Saturday.'

Simon pulled a silk handkerchief from his pocket and wiped his face. It was pale and exhausted. Joan could see his tall body shaking. And she thought:

'He does love me, just as I love him. My darling precious Simon. I can't fight him much longer! It's too much like hard work, fighting myself, too.'

Said Simon:

'Very well. One more week, Joan. Seven days and nights of hell away from each other. Then we'll make our decision.'

Joan drew her coat around her and buttoned it. Her own fingers were trembling as she tried to smooth back her disordered hair and searched frantically for a pin with which to fasten a dark lock that Simon's passionate fingers had loosened.

Sally's voice, a little fractious now, cut like a sword between them.

'Simon, where the dickens are you?'

He seized Joan's hand, and carried it to his lips. Lips feverish and burning against her palm.

'Good-bye, my love.'

'Good-bye,' she whispered back and wished

that her heart would not turn over when he touched her, spoke to her like that.

Then he was gone. Gone toward Sally and duty, out of the shadows into the moonlight where Sally waited for him. But Joan knew that he was leaving all that mattered to him here with her, in the green gloom of this hiding-place.

She turned to the stone nymph, put her warm palm—the one he had just kissed—against the cold feet of the statue. She looked up at that frightened sculptured face and said under her breath:

'What shall I do? What did *you* do in the end? Did your lover catch you and hold you forever? I wonder! I wonder if in the dim ages back that stone heart of yours ever beat as mine beats when Simon kisses me!'

But the stone nymph had no answer for that warm human supplicant, and after a moment Joan laughed at herself for being so foolish and began to retrace her footsteps back to the hotel.

She intended to slip in by a back entrance in order that she should not risk meeting Simon or Sally. But there was to be no respite for her tonight. She ran straight into them. They were walking arm-in-arm down the path that led to the cloisters. It could not but give Joan a pang to see Sally's radiant white figure, jewels glittering in her ears and round her throat . . . Sally, hanging on to Simon, laughing up at him, enjoying his company as she had a right to do. And at the same time Joan was conscious of strange relief because Simon was not laughing at Sally. He walked with his face grimly set, staring in front of him.

Joan tried to slip by but Sally saw her.

'Hello, Joan! You old meanie! I thought you were going to bed. Why didn't you join us for the dance!'

Joan avoided Simon's gaze. She said:

'I'm just off to bed now. I was taking a walk.'

'A pity you didn't take it with Simon. He's been doing a moonlight flit from me,' said Sally.

Then Joan glanced through her lashes at Simon. Did those gay, friendly words make him feel guilty? No, his face remained stony. He showed no signs of conscience. But Joan felt relieved that she had not driven that smile from Sally's face, yet if only she would say something unkind . . . if only she were a little rotter . . . anything . . . so that they would have the right to desert her and make her unhappy . . . but they hadn't, they had no right, and what was the use of waiting this week anyhow? The doubts and agonies would only start all over again when Simon came back to Great Friars.

Joan, feeling frustrated and desperate, muttered a few words, bade Sally and Simon a hasty good night, then left them there, feeling that she had stood quite enough for one night.

68

Sally looked after Joan's retreating form.

'That girl's working too hard, don't you think?'

'Maybe,' said Simon, his face not losing its rigid look.

Sally walked him down to the cloisters. Once away from the lights of the hotel and in the seclusion of the old stone archways, she slipped an arm round his neck and became soft and yielding, which was rare for Sally.

'I haven't had a real kiss all day,' she murmured.

His fingers clenched. He could dance with Sally, talk and argue with her, force himself to be gay with her. But make love to her he could not. Not tonight anyhow, with Joan's kiss still warm upon his lips.

He touched Sally's fair hair.

'It would be a pity to spoil your make-up, and I must say you are looking lovely,' he said with a flippant air.

But Sally, as luck would have it, was in no flippant mood. She wanted to be petted and spoiled. And what Sally wanted she must have.

She let the summer-ermine cape which she was wearing slide a little off her beautiful bare shoulders. The scent which she used was strong, too strong for Simon's liking. He was always telling her so. (Ah, but the perfume of Joan's hair had been like new-mown hay with the sun on it. Fresh and clean and wholesome.)

'Give me a little kiss,' Sally whispered, and

rubbed her cheek against his chin.

Mechanically his arms went around her. He had the wildest desire to tell her about Joan, here and now, and put an end to this farce. But he had promised Joan to wait a week, so a week he must wait. But never before had he known more conclusively that he could not make Sally his wife. His passion for her was dead. Only affection remained, and gratitude for the favours she had shown him. It was Joan whom he loved and Joan whom he must marry, else stay alone for the rest of his life.

Sally stirred restlessly in his arms.

'Where's my kiss?'

He temporised.

'Darling, I've got the devil of a headache.' Then, when she started to sympathise and to stroke his hair, he felt immensely irritated both with her and himself. What a feeble feminine prevarication in order to escape a caress! He felt that it would have been more manly to have told her the truth right away. He felt annoyed even with Joan, because she forced him to eke out the agony. Although he knew, of course, that she was trying to put up a fight, and that was both sweet and generous of her. But it was also futile.

He saw before him a week of nerves and depression. A week in which he wanted to work hard, too, and to put his mind to earning his living. He was so sick of being useless, of frittering away both time and energy. But little hope was there of thinking about anything next week except Joan and the ultimate drama of their decision. A decision which he knew even now must be made in favour of Joan and himself. She, like himself, must accept their love as the inevitable.

Sally did not get her long, lover's kiss. She had to be content with the touch of his lips on her hair, the pressure of his hand, and an apology for his *malaise.*

She thought she knew Simon pretty well. He was not as easy-going as she was. He was moody, difficult at times. But it amused her to cope with his difficult moments. She was immensely vain. She liked to flatter herself that she could do anything with a man. Even with Simon who was no ordinary being. At times she had to confess to herself that he scared her a little. He could be so brutally cynical and censorious. But it excited her when she managed to rouse physical response from him. If she could not reach his mental level, she was not particularly disappointed. She never worried herself with the mental or spiritual side. She was essentially material. And so long as Simon made love to her, she believed that he loved her. If he did not, she took it for granted that he was in a bad mood but not fed up with her. After all, she could not accuse him of neglect. He had spoiled and petted her since their engagement to an extent which satisfied her.

Neither was Sally fundamentally jealous. She considered that Simon belonged to her but she would not really have minded had he chosen to flirt a bit with another woman, any more than she would expect him to mind if she indulged in a 'good time' with some boy friend. It wouldn't mean anything.

'Terribly sorry poor Big Boy's got a howwid headache,' she said in a baby voice. It was a voice which Simon never cared for and tonight he could hardly bear it.

'Think I'll turn in if you don't mind,' he said abruptly and drew away from her, suffocated by so much perfume and sweetness.

'Oh!' said Sally, disappointed, 'No more dancing?'

'If you like, one more.'

'Sure the head's not too bad?'

'No, come along,' he said, trying to be pleasant. Sally was so like a child, anxious for a good time and hurt when she did not get one. That was strange. She could be hard and *blasé,* yet ridiculously young. In one way she had never really grown up. She never would grow up. Never be a thinking, grand woman like Joan. Joan who was just as young in years as Sally.

In the dance room they ran into a fair young man with a gardenia in his buttonhole, and horn-rimmed glasses. He looked flushed and happy and quite inane. He greeted Sally uproariously.

72

'Whoopee! It's our Sally. Simon, old boy, stand aside in favour of one who adores your affianced wife, shamelessly. *Quite* shamelessly, my boy!'

Simon stood aside more swiftly and gladly perhaps than was discreet. This was the Hon. Keith Dettering, more commonly known in his set at Koko. He had the brains of a rabbit, an ideally happy disposition, and an income which enabled him to spend his money and his time flying his Moth plane, or driving his powerful Hispano Suiza from one society playground to the other.

He was of a type which sickened Simon and yet he had allowed himself to become one of that set. And that had begun to sicken him, too. That was what he had tired of now. The fruitless chase from the Ritz bar in London to the Ritz bar in Paris. From Venice and the Lido to the Sporting Club at Monte Carlo or Juan les Pins, running up bills he could ill afford in order to keep up the pace with one of Koko's income. That was what Sally expected him to do in future on *her* income, and the very idea nauseated him. He wondered why in heaven's name he had ever allowed himself to be drawn into the net. He wondered, too, why Sally had not chosen to marry a man like Koko who could give her an Earl for a father-in-law.

Sally was quite fond of Koko. She liked to play with him. She now held out both hands with a dramatic gesture and said:

'*Monsieur*, I am yours. My future spouse has the *migraine* and is withdrawing from the party.'

'Whoopee!' said the Hon. Koko. 'But for a fellow to relinquish the side of any girl as gorgeous as yourself, there can be no punishment too great. I suggest that you break your engagement with Simon and marry me.'

Simon smiled. But behind the smile there was bitter irritation, a sense of complete frustration. It was so like that young fool to voice in jest what he, Simon, wished were a living truth.

Sally gave her high peal of laughter and took the hand that Mr. Dettering extended.

'I will consider the suggestion, but I'm not sure I want to exchange my bottle of champagne here . . .' she nudged Simon affectionately . . . 'for a cup of cocoa.'

'You're tight, darling,' said Koko, 'or you would never allow yourself to utter that old, worn-out pun.'

Sally put her hand to her ear.

'Hark! Methinks they are playing the strains of my favourite rumba. Come on, Koko, let's show them how it's done in South America!'

Koko waggled his body and clicked his fingers in imitation of castanets. At the same time he hummed a few words of the tune that the band was playing. Sally unhooked her fur cape, flung it at Simon, and glided into Koko's arms. They began to execute the dance with great solemnity and some grace for Koko was an excellent dancer.

'Night-night, darling!' sang out Sally. 'Mind the poor head's better in the morning.'

'Swallow a bottle of aspirin, old boy,' sang out Koko grinning over Sally's shoulder.

Sick at heart Simon turned away. He walked up to a page, handed him the cape and told him to send it up to Miss Vaughan's suite. Then he took the lift to his own room.

Almost savagely he drew the white carnation from his buttonhole and flung it into the wastepaper basket. The story of his headache was no longer a lie. His temples were throbbing furiously. He retained a picture of Sally and Koko dancing their rumba. Sally, all smiles and dimples, thoroughly enjoying herself. God! How had he in his wildest dreams ever imagined that she would make the right wife for him. Why had he allowed himself to be influenced by the thought of her money or her charm. It was a charm which would eventually stifle a man—a man who was at all serious-minded. It was Koko whom she should have married. Why didn't she fall in love with him? Even now she must realise in time that he, Simon Roxley, was not in any way as well suited to be her husband as Dettering.

Sitting on the edge of his bed, Simon let his hot head fall into his hands. And now he thought of Joan, lovely and soothing, with her low voice, her wide, tranquil eyes. It was Joan whom he must choose and with whom he must go to the end of the world if need be. Surely, eventually Sally would forget her feeling for him and find her title, her happiness, as the Hon. Mrs. Keith Dettering? But whatever she did he could not reconsider his decision to break with her and marry Joan.

He wondered how he could get through this next week. He hoped to heaven Sally would not be too demanding, or drag him into too many parties. Fortunately he could give the excuse that he was working and needed early nights. But he wished, in a way, that he could go down to his father's home. He needed the peace and dignity of the old place. Unfortunately he was too far out of town. He had to stay in his club in Pall Mall.

He made up his mind to be strong and not see Joan again before he left Great Friars. But before he went to bed, he sat at the desk and wrote a note to her. He half-smiled as he sealed the envelope. For the very fact that he was ready to put down his feelings in black and white was proof to him that he loved her. He, the cautious Simon, who had written to no woman in terms of love until he became engaged to Sally. He felt indeed that the die was already cast and the battle over, once he had penned those words: *'I love you, Joan, now, until death and after that!'*

Joan read that poignant line the following morning. (It was sent up to her room early before even she had the chance to get downstairs.) Sitting up in bed, wide awake, she read and read every word he had written. Simon had left the hotel. He said that by the time she received his letter he would be well away in his car *en route* for London. And he said a great many other things, all assuring her that although he would do his utmost to make this week a time of trial, a period during which he would give every thought to the position, and be as fair to Sally as he could, he knew it was a waste of time. He could and would marry nobody else but her, Joan. He felt that she could not possibly be doing the right thing by sending him away when both of them felt as they did about each other.

His method of signature left Joan with a thudding heart and flaming cheeks.

'Your Simon.'

Hers! Heavens! If that were only true. But it wasn't. He had no right to sign such a thing. He was Sally's. And she, Joan, must not be betrayed from her feelings of loyalty and honour by this wild leaping of her blood at every word from him, every memory of his embrace.

This week *should* be a fair trial. She would not answer that letter. She would not allow her mind to wander to Simon. She would be a prig, a prude, anything rather than what she really was, just a woman wildly and exquisitely in love.

Down went Joan to her work of the day. She threw herself into it with more zeal than usual. The harder she worked, the better. There were many things to be done. The hotel would be emptying this morning of some of its visitors who were only 'week-enders'. Her post showed that there were two fresh bookings, and her diary reminded her that Major and Mrs. Collier were arriving from Aldershot for a week. She must remember to tell the head chambermaid to get the blue tapestry bedroom ready for the Colliers. And that nice couple, the Merrimans, with their Nanny and two babies would be leaving this morning, too. She would miss the small four-year-old boy, David. He often met her coming in from his morning walk and rushed up to her with shouts of joy because once she had taken him on the river with Ham, and he had never forgotten the excitement of such a treat.

Joan was devoted to small children. She knew that when she married she would want children. Simon would want them too. But Sally—Sally might regard it as her duty to provide the Roxleys with an heir, and after that no more. There were no real maternal instincts in her.

Joan wished that she had not to see Sally again, this morning, but of course Sally had no intention of getting up as early as Simon. She had planned to go up to town with her friend, Koko, in his new Dussenberg, which was one

78

of the most powerful racing cars he had ever driven. Sally loved it. Speed was one of her manias!

Fortunately for Joan she was spared the embarrassment of too long and private a talk with her employer. Miss Vaughan, as was her habit, got up at the last possible moment, and left everything so late that she only had time to discuss the affairs of the hotel in the most superficial manner.

'I leave everything to you, darling,' she told Joan as she left. 'And Simon says the place must be paying handsomely, so what more could we want? You're a wonder. I couldn't do without you. Bye-bye till next week-end.'

The praise merely heaped coals of fire on Joan's head. She was miserable for a long while after Sally had gone. Having made up her mind not to think of Simon, she thought of little else, and in her was the ever-growing conviction that it would be impossible for them to let Sally down.

After lunch, just as she was going off duty and leaving her secretary, Miss Anderson, in charge of the office, Joan was plunged into a domestic crisis.

One of the chambermaids appeared with reddened eyelids and sullen mouth, and gave in her notice.

She asked to speak to Miss Parwood alone. Miss Anderson retired and left them together. Joan questioned the girl with some surprise.

Doris Homer was one of her best maids, a pretty girl and a popular one.

'Why, Doris,' said Joan, 'unless you have any serious reason for wishing to leave at once, I hope you'll reconsider it. This is just our busiest season and you know I have always relied on you.'

Doris sniffed.

'I'm not staying to be treated anyhow by Bert Freeman.'

For an instant Joan was perplexed. Freeman? Then she remembered that he was the second chef in the hotel. And as far as she could remember, he was quite a nice young man.

Of course it was nothing new for there to be trouble between the two sexes in the hotel staff. And the story that Doris blurted out was the usual one. Bert had been making unwelcome advances. Doris didn't care for Bert and so upon Joan's shoulders must fall the extra work and annoyance of having to find a new chambermaid at a moment's notice.

Joan, in her tactful, sympathetic way, managed to induce the angry Doris to give the matter another chance, on condition that Bert was spoken to. So, after her departure, the second chef was sent for, and made his appearance in the office.

Joan, sitting at her desk in her fresh green linen overall, looked far too young and lovely to be dealing with situations of the kind. But

80

Mr. Bert Freeman, like most of the staff, had a wholesome respect for Miss Parwood. And what protest he had to make, he made quite politely.

'Begging your pardon, miss, the fault's not on one side. I'd as lief have paid attention to one of the frying pans as Doris Homer if I'd known there was any objection. But it was she who started it and I'm telling you the truth, miss, and you can ask the others if she didn't make a set at me before I give her so much as a look.'

Joan drew pictures on her blotter and tried not to smile. It was rather funny. At the same time it was rather sad. All this sex . . . it made life so difficult. Either the man after the girl or the girl after the man, and invariably to no purpose.

A few soothing words and some advice to Bert, who was a nice-looking boy with no real harm in him, and the second chef retired to the kitchen determined not to pay court to any of the girls in the hotel whether they 'made a set at him' or not.

'I don't understand girls, miss, and I don't want to,' was his final remark to Joan.

After he had gone, Joan said to herself:

'And I don't understand men—or myself. What's the use of trying? It's just that one feels this and that, and feelings are the very devil— they run away with one, no matter how hard one tries to be good. Oh, Simon, Simon, *what's*

81

going to happen to us on Sunday?'

CHAPTER EIGHT

Those five days between Monday and Saturday seemed to Joan the longest and yet the shortest she had ever known. In one way they dragged. It seemed as though a sudden barrier had sprung up between Simon and herself. A wall of silence. They had agreed not to write to each other. She wondered what he was doing in town. How many dances or parties he would go to with Sally. What his feelings were, now that he was away from her, Joan. For all she knew, the week-end might just have been a temporary lapse, a mad infatuation on his part. Up in town with Sally and his friends, he might regret what he had done and be perfectly ready to carry on with his marriage.

And in one way the week went too quickly for Joan. She dreaded Simon's return. Alternated between praying that he had not ceased to love her, and hoping for Sally's sake that they would have the strength to give each other up, when they met again.

She was a nervous wreck by the time that week ended. There were hotel worries for her as well. Having got over the little drama of Bert and Doris, Joan had to cope with one of the pantry boys who developed a septic finger and had to go home. Then one of the staff started colds, and in several cases Joan had to dose the girls with aspirin, hot whisky and lemon, and pray that they would not spread the germs through the hotel. It was the treacherous June weather. Last week-end it had been blazing hot. This Saturday dawned chilly and it was pouring with rain. Which meant that some of the weekenders would cancel, that fires must be lit in the big hall, and that the visitors instead of being able to get out into the beautiful gardens, or on the river, would group in the lounges, grousing and not knowing what to do with themselves. There was nothing Joan dreaded more than a spirit of discontent in the hotel. So many people were apt to get bored and blame Great Friars for it rather than the weather. That was bad for business.

The grey skies and sodden flowers did not help to lighten Joan's spirits on this day which was to be one of the most crucial in her life. From the moment that she awoke, she felt terrified about the future. It frightened her to think of what would happen if Simon was still determined to marry her. It frightened her to think of what would happen if he was not, and she had to leave her job, leave *him* whom she loved more than anybody in the world! Immediately after breakfast she went out. New curtains and covers were being put in the little writing-room next to the cocktail bar. The green chintzes of last year had faded abominably. Sally had asked her to go into Maidenhead and choose some patterns for her to see when she came down. She was not arriving with Simon today. He had gone down to his father's place last night and would motor here by himself. Sally was coming with a party of friends, including the faithful Koko.

Joan, whose heart seemed to have been beating fast and painfully the whole morning, felt positively breathless as she wondered which one of them would get here first. She hoped to God it would be Simon. It would be so much better to get their discussion over before Sally came. Yet how could they sit down and say, in cold blood, either: 'We *will tell Sally the truth*,' or 'We *will say good-bye.*' It was unthinkable. Her world was upside down. The knowledge that Simon loved her and that she cared so desperately for him had shattered her peace of mind for ever. Yet only a few weeks ago she had been here at her job serenely, at peace, happy in a fashion. Oh, not wildly happy as she might have been with him, but content as one is content with an ordinary prosaic existence before knowing anything better.

Joan rang up the garage for a car to take her into Maidenhead. William Hamley, himself, elected to fetch her in his own coupé.

'You oughn't to bother,' Joan said as she took her place beside him. 'I'm sure you should stay at the garage, Ham.'

He answered:

'I've scarcely seen you the whole week. They can get on with things alone at the garage for an hour. What the dickens have you been doing with yourself, Joan? Every time I've 'phoned, you've been busy. If I've called, you've sent a message to say you're somewhere else. Have you been deliberately avoiding me?'

'Of course not, silly,' she said. But her cheeks coloured a trifle guiltily. It was true that she had been avoiding dear old Ham. The week had been so chaotic, so fraught with tension and thoughts of Simon, she had not wanted to see even her best friend. And Ham was in love with her. He would soon detect that something was wrong. And he would be blunt enough to comment upon it. Which he did before they were a few miles away from the hotel.

'Look here, Joan, you're looking ill—as though you haven't slept for nights. What on earth's the matter? What's going on?'

'Nothing,' she said, wondering how she could lie so shamelessly.

To her dismay, he pulled the car up on the side of the road and stopped the windscreen wiper which was droning to and fro. The wind was driving the rain in sheets against the windows of the car. Joan, in spite of the rug which Ham had tucked around her knees, shivered. She felt his gaze upon her but would not look at him.

'Joan,' he said. 'We're pals, aren't we?'

'Of course.'

'Then please tell me what's troubling you. Something's very wrong and I want to know about it—to help if I can.'

She shook her head mutely. His bright blue eyes regarded her with grave concern. It was true that she was looking ill. Pale cheeks, dark circled eyes. None of her usual buoyancy and humour. Not a smile, and Joan was always one for a joke. Yet how lovely she was in that grey flannel suit, pale yellow linen blouse and the grey felt hat on the side of her smooth dark head. He adored her. He'd give anything to drive that suffering look out of her face.

What was it? Something to do with that fellow, Roxley, Ham was certain.

Then, suddenly, in desperation, almost at the end of her tether, Joan turned to him.

'I'll tell you something, Ham. I'll tell you about a friend of mine. It's—it's her trouble. It's worrying me . . .' she stammered. 'And I want some advice for her. You see, my friend is in love with a man who—is going to marry another girl. The man's in love with my—my friend, too.'

'Well . . .' asked Ham gently, as she paused.

'Well, do you think that those two have the right to go off together—the right to break the heart of the girl to whom the man's engaged?'

Ham took a packet of cigarettes from his

86

pocket, lit one and sat back in the corner of the car.

'If it's real love and not infatuation, it's quite right. It would be wrong for the man to marry the girl he didn't love. He'd only break her heart another way, in the long run.'

Joan was ashamed of the eagerness with which she clung to those words. She felt that she did, indeed, need support, some outsider to vindicate her action if she was going to surrender.

'Do you think they ought to tell the girl at once?'

'The sooner the better. Any man who marries a girl just because he's engaged to her and thinks he ought to, when he's stopped caring for her, is crazy.'

'But there's a little more to it than that,' added Joan. 'My—my friend owes rather a lot to this girl and . .

'Oh, cut it out, Joan,' broke in Ham with a crudeness born of his sudden, fierce jealousy. 'You needn't hedge with me. You're talking of yourself, aren't you? Yourself and Simon Roxley?'

Down went Joan's defences. Her head sank and she put a small gloved hand up to her eyes.

'Oh, God!' she said miserably.

She felt Ham's hand on her knee.

'You needn't mind me knowing, Joan. You know I'd never breathe a word to anybody.'

'I know,' she whispered. 'But Ham, it's so awful!'

'I can't say it amuses me . . . when you know how I feel about you'

'I'm terribly sorry.'

'You needn't be. At least, you can be if you like. I don't object to a little sympathy.'

She tried to laugh and ended on the note of a sob. 'I could sympathise with anybody on earth who's in love—hopelessly in love.'

'From what you've just been saying, it can't be so hopeless for you. Roxley's in love with you.'

'How on earth did you guess?'

He smoked furiously for a second and then said:

'It's pretty obvious. I've seen you look at each other. I've guessed for some time that you've been keen, and I'm not surprised he prefers you to Miss Vaughan.'

'She's lovely and . . .

'Not my idea of lovely,' broke in Ham. 'And not Mr. Roxley's either, so it seems.'

'But there's so much at stake, Ham. He ought to marry her.'

'He's after the money, isn't he?'

'Don't make it sound so crude.'

'Sorry. Isn't it a fact?'

'Not altogether. He was quite in love with her when they became engaged. Naturally he needed money because of the family and the estate, but now he's willing to give up everything—for me.'

William Hamley looked at Joan's profile. For an instant stark pain lay in his nice blue eyes.

'Wouldn't any man on earth give up everything for you, Joan? I know I would.'

She looked up at him, tears on her lashes.

'Bless you, Ham. You're so nice to me and you make me so ashamed. I don't know what you must think of me . . .'

'What I thought of you before. There's no one to touch you. You couldn't help falling in love with this bloke. And I know darn well he couldn't help falling for you. Neither could I.'

'And you really think we ought to tell Sally?'

'I'm afraid I do, although the last thing I want to see is you married to someone else.'

She drew her hand across her forehead and gave a long sigh.

'It's all—awful. I shall be thankful when today's over I couldn't bear much more of this sort of suspense. I've been trying to do the right thing, Ham.'

He took her hand and pressed it in sympathy.

'I bet you have, poor kid.'

'But I'm afraid I shall give in. I'm terribly in love with him, Ham.'

'You'd be a fool not to take your happiness. If I know Miss Vaughan, she'll get over it. You wouldn't.'

'He is—rather marvellous.'

'Darned attractive. I must say I've always liked him,' said Ham a bit grudgingly. 'And so you, little Joan, will one day be Lady Roxley, hey? Sounds a bit more glamorous than Mrs. William Hamley, I must admit.'

'Oh, don't!' said Joan gulping. 'It hasn't come off yet.'

'It will. That's what Roxley's coming down for today, isn't it? To settle things with you.'

'I suppose so,' said Joan, and stared in a dazed way out at the rain and at the wet road before them.

'Well, you know I wish you the best of luck, and you know if ever there's anything I can do for you, I'll do it.'

'You're a perfect dear,' she whispered, and suddenly, impulsively, leaned upwards and touched his cheek with her lips.

He caught fire at the contact with her, put both arms about her and kissed her full on the lips. When he drew back, his face was fiery red.

'It's the first time I've ever done that and it will probably be the last, so I hope you don't mind.'

Dumbly she shook her head. He switched on the engine and they began to move towards Maidenhead. For a long while she sat silent and unhappy. Conscious of the fact that she was unwittingly hurting this nice, honest young man. But she could not help it. Could not feel a thrill at his kiss. Hadn't a poet once said with truth: *'How is it in our power to love or not to love?*" Well, it was out of their power. Out of hers to stop loving Simon and to love Ham. Out of Ham's power, perhaps, to stop loving her. It was all so sad and difficult.

But somehow she was relieved and glad to have had that little talk with Ham. What he had said did at least confirm her belief that she had the right to take this love which Simon offered. (That is, if he came down here today and offered it again.) Albeit she was still terribly conscious of disloyalty to her friend.

The morning went on.

After lunch the weather cleared a little. Some sunlight broke through the struggling clouds. The barometer in the entrance hall was going up. The gloom of the early day which had descended upon the guests lifted. Everybody seemed hopeful for a fine afternoon.

Joan wondered if it was an augury. Yet as far as she could see there was little ahead of her but storms.

After lunch she stayed in her office writing letters, trying to concentrate on her job. But every time the door opened her head shot up and her heart missed a beat. Was it Simon—or Sally!

It was Simon who came first. Not into her office. The first intimation that she had of his arrival was three lines scribbled on Great Friars notepaper and brought to her by Wilkins, the page.

'I am here in Sally's sitting-room. Please come to me, darling.
Simon.'

Then Joan knew that the hour was upon her—the hour of the most momentous decision of her life. And now love must either win or lose.

There was no colour in her face at all when she opened the door of Sally's private sitting-room, which was on the first floor, facing the river. Earlier this morning Joan had decorated it with masses of blue lupins and pink roses.

Her hand shook so that she could scarcely turn the handle.

She walked in and stood with her back to the door, breathing fast. She saw Simon by the window with a shaft of sunlight falling upon him. Tall, graceful Simon, with his proud black head and his sloe-black eyes. An eager bright face he turned to her. So full of radiant anticipation was that face that she knew as soon as she looked at him that he had not changed, and that his mind was made up. Then with three giant strides, he was across the flower-filled room and had her in his arms. Wordlessly he held her, kissed her with kisses that left her no power to fight them, no wish indeed, to fight any longer. She was all his and she knew it. She said so with her arms locked around his neck.

'It's no good, Simon. If you want me I've got to come to you. I know it,' she said.

'Darling,' he said, 'thank God. I know it too. I've known it the whole of this week. What a hell of a week—away from you—wanting you, my sweet, my *sweet*.'

She was near to fainting then. He felt her small slim body sag in his arms. He picked her up and carried her to the deep-cushioned Chesterfield which was opposite the fire. He sat there with her in his arms, and kissed the colour back to her face and the stars to her eyes.

For a long while she was unable to speak or move. With the blood pounding in her temples and every instinct in her responding to the passion of this man whom she knew was indubitably hers, she could not even remember Sally.

And when she did remember and drew away from Simon's possessive arms, she sat there, face hidden in her hands and thought:

'I can't help it. It's beyond me. It's beyond you, Simon. We can neither of us fight a thing like this. Sally must be told.'

Simon, one hand fast locked in hers, drew a sigh like a man who has been drowning and just reached the surface of the water again.

'Well, thank heavens, we've both reached the same decision, my sweet.'

'And now what do we do?'

He let go her hand, stood up, walked to the

93

windows, and looked down at the gardens. Two girls in shorts and carrying tennis racquets were walking over the wet lawn towards the hard courts. The sun having banished the grey skies of the morning, was shining bravely. Simon caught a glimpse of the sparkling river, and the flash of a scarlet Japanese umbrella, as a punt drifted by. It was a gay and lovely world. He felt that with Joan as his wife, it would be a lovelier world than he had ever believed possible. At the same time there was a pang in his heart because of Sally. A pang because he was going to hurt her. A twinge of remorse because he was backing out of a commitment. He didn't like doing that. But it was inevitable. All these days and nights with Sally in town, he had tried to make himself believe that he could say good-bye to Joan and go through with his marriage. But it was hopeless. If he married Sally he would only make her miserable. She would soon realise that he was no longer in love with her. In telling the truth he was doing the right thing.

He turned back to Joan. She was dabbing a powder-puff over her face and straightening her hair. Her gaze met his. She smiled. That smile, and all that it meant, strengthened Simon.

With two strides he was back beside her, carrying both her hands to his lips.

'Lovely thing! Don't worry! It's going to be all right. Sally's not unreasonable. She may

94

take it badly to begin with, but she'll soon realise it's for the best!'

Joan sighed.

'What will she think of me—after all she's done!'

'She'll forgive you. I'll tell her I made you do it.'

'You needn't. I'd like to take my own share of the guilt—if guilt it is.'

'I don't see why we should feel guilty. We couldn't help falling in love, Joan.'

'Well, it's no good talking about it any more. We've made up our minds and we must act quickly now. But Simon, it's your family I'm worrying about. That father and brother of yours—they'll be terribly disappointed. I'm bringing you nothing—not a cent—I'm simply an employee of Miss Vaughan's.'

'You're the woman I love, Joan. When I tell my father and brother so, it'll be good enough for them. They can't expect me to bolster them up at the cost of my own personal happiness. It would be damned selfish if they did.'

Somebody knocked on the door.

'Miss Parwood, please.'

Joan sprang up.

That's the page. I expect I'm wanted. I'm on duty, you know, Simon.'

His dark eyes followed her as she walked to the door. He waited until she had spoken to the page, and then called her back.

'When shall I see you again?'

'As soon as Sally comes. We must get that over.'

'Then there'll be a bit of a mess! You won't want to stay in the hotel, and Sally won't want you to go until she's found a substitute, and—well—the best thing for me to do is to leave, tonight.'

Joan's straight brows drew together. Passionately—in love though she was, her sense of duty was still strong.

'I couldn't leave Sally in a hole. I must stay here until she finds someone else.'

'There couldn't be a second Joan.'

'There are dozens,' she smiled. Then added: 'I suppose poor Sally will rush away from Great Friars, too. Oh, I *do* hope she won't be too miserable. Simon, I loathe to feel we're going to make her miserable!'

'So do I, but don't change your mind about me, for God's sake.'

'No,' she said, looking him straight in the eyes. 'I couldn't do that—*now*.'

The telephone bell rang sharply in Sally's sitting room.

'I'll answer it,' said Joan.

She put the receiver to her ear. Simon, taking a cigarette from the little Georgian snuff box which he used for a case, heard her say:

'What is it? Who is it? The *police*? But what about? . . . an accident . . . good God! Yes, yes . . . switch it through at once . . .'

The cigarette remained unlit. Joan turned to Simon with a face drained of colour.

'What is it?' he asked her.

'It's an accident. It seems to be . . . Sally . . .'

'Sally!' repeated Simon. 'But good heavens, where? How?'

'I don't know. They're just switching the police through. I'll know in a minute.'

He looked at his wrist watch.

'Let me think . . . she was coming down with Koko and Diana Croydon and some other fellow . . . in Koko's car . . .'

Joan turned back to the telephone.

'Hullo! Hullo, yes? This is Miss Parwood speaking. You want Mr. Roxley? Very well. Hold on. Here he is.'

She thrust the white ivory instrument into Simon's hand and stood there, quaking, dreading what he was to hear and she was soon to know. She gathered little from what he said. But when he put the instrument back on its rest and turned to her, she saw that he was badly shaken. There was a grey look on his face.

'Oh, what is it, Simon? Tell me quickly.'

'The little fool!' he said in a tone of despair. 'Oh, the *little fool*! I always told her not to go up with that imbecile, Koko.'

'Go up where?'

'In his plane. He flies a Puss-Moth. Apparently she didn't start out from town by car. You know what they all are—always full of

97

wild ideas. At the last moment Koko suggested flying Sally down to Bourne End, then having his chauffeur meet them and bring them on here. He got into a tail-spin just before they landed at Cockmarsh. If they'd come down anywhere else, they'd probably both be dead.'

'What's happened?'

'Koko's only cut and bruised. But Sally . . . God! poor Sally!'

Joan felt the blood ebb from her very heart. 'Well?'

'Well, they say that it's her eyes. She's been taken to hospital. They don't know the extent of the injuries yet. But the men who gave her first aid seem to think that she—she'd been blinded by the crash.'

A moment's silence. Joan heard the tick-tick of the little glass clock on Sally's writing-table. And, from the gardens came the gay laugh of a child. Joan felt that it was one of the worst moments of her life, as she stood there, staring into Simon's eyes. The shock of this news was almost paralysing. She could hardly think. It couldn't be true that Sally had crashed at the landing ground and that her sight had gone. *Her sight gone*. That, of course, was exaggerated. It *couldn't* be true! They couldn't know, without a proper examination. Joan found herself saying so aloud, wildly, to Simon. But at the same time she had the awful feeling that while Sally had been involved in a frightful accident, she, Joan, and

98

Simon had been planning to rob Sally of her future husband and her happiness. It wasn't a pleasant thought.

Simon said:

'I know what you're thinking. But don't! You mustn't! We were going to do the right thing, Joan, in owning up to the truth.'

'Well, we can't tell her now.'

'Not at the moment, of course. We'll go straight to the hospital together. I'll drive you. As you say, things may not be nearly so bad as they're painted.'

Joan gave a shudder.

'One couldn't think of Sally as blind—her eyes are her best feature—so full of life . . . '

'We must go to her,' interrupted Simon.

Joan held out a hand to him. She had never needed the strength and warmth of his fingers more. A few moments ago she had been sitting there on that Chesterfield, ecstatic, seizing her happiness, believing that everything was going to be all right. And now this . . . this accident to Sally which made it impossible for Simon to break his engagement.

He put an arm about her and led her to the door.

'Don't look like that, darling. You mustn't. It only means delaying things for a few days, perhaps.'

'I wonder,' said Joan in a hollow voice. 'I wonder if we'll ever be able to tell her about us—*now!*'

CHAPTER NINE

Within the next hour, Joan and Simon knew the worst. The unfortunate Koko was there at the hospital to greet them. He had escaped miraculously, and had been able to climb out of the cockpit with help. Except for some strips of plaster on his cheek, and a bandage round his head, he seemed little the worse. He was up and dressed and capable of talking to the pair who arrived from Great Friars.

But it was a very shaken and agonised Koko, roused from his inanity at last by the seriousness of the thing he had done.

'It's appalling, old man,' he said hoarsely to Simon as he faced Sally's fiancé and friend in the matron's sitting-room. 'I wish to God I'd died before this happened. I can't think how it *did* happen. We were just over Cockmarsh—it's the A.A. landing-place at Bourne End. Then the spin . . . it was horrible, old fellow . . . and I don't remember much else until I was helped out of the plane. I saw Sally . . . her white helmet covered in blood . . . oh God!' He hid his face in his hands and burst into tears.

Joan, sick at heart, tried to comfort him. Simon listened stonily to the boy's hysterical sobs. Koko kept moaning:

'I adore Sally. I wouldn't have had it happen for the world. Her beautiful eyes. Oh God!'

The matron spoke quietly to Simon.

'I must be frank with you, Mr. Roxley. There's little hope for Miss Vaughan's sight. She got the worst of this crash, I'm afraid.'

'She must have every attention—the best specialists,' said Simon hoarsely.

The matron nodded.

She could see that money was no object here and was duly impressed by the fact that the young pilot was an earl's son, that Sally was the well-known proprietress of Great Friars, and that her fiancé was Sir George Roxley's heir.

'Naturally everything will be done,' she said, 'and we will help you. So far, Miss Vaughan has seen our visiting ophthalmic surgeon, Mr. Fisher-West. who has done wonderful work here. He thinks it's the optic nerve which was destroyed in the crash.'

Simon turned to Joan. She had left Koko who had collapsed in a chair, sobbing quietly to himself.

Poor devil, thought Simon. One had to feel sorry for him. It must be awful to feel one was responsible for such a thing.

Joan said:

'Let's go and see Sally, Simon.'

He nodded.

'Yes.

The matron herself conducted them to the private room in which Sally Vaughan was lying. Up till now she had been conscious, and in acute agony with her injured eyes. Now she was succumbing to the merciful relief afforded by an injection of morphia.

Simon was never very good in sick-rooms, and it cost him an effort to enter this one with its odour of antiseptics. It was all so clean, so bare, so dim. So starkly unlike the sort of room that Sally liked, with flowers and gay colours and an atmosphere full of fun. Mechanically, Simon reminded himself to send masses of flowers and almost immediately there followed the appalling thought that *she wouldn't be able to see them.* It didn't matter where she was lying. She couldn't see. She might as well be in her own luxurious bedroom as here, in this narrow one at the hospital.

Together Simon and Joan came to Sally's bedside, both reluctant to look down and see the havoc wrought by the accident. But there was nothing unsightly about the girl who lay there in that white narrow bed. By some miracle her face had escaped. It looked particularly beautiful in its marble pallor. A bandage covered her golden hair like a cap, and there were bandages over her eyes. It gave her almost a nun-like appearance. She was a strange, unrecognisable Sally without the bright scarlet rouge which had been wiped from her lips.

Neither Joan nor Simon had any thought for themselves in that moment. They concentrated upon her. She was not yet sleeping. Her hands groped restlessly. Just the same slender hands with their scarlet-varnished nails, and on the engagement finger, Simon's ring, the big sparkling emerald set in diamonds which she had chosen.

The very sight of that ring gave Joan a pang. Had this accident not occurred, that ring might by now have been removed from that finger. But there it was still, and Sally was very much Simon's, still. Simon was saying:

'Sally, darling, my poor little Sally . . .'

The injured girl turned her piteous swathed head in his direction.

'Simon . . . Simon . . .' she whispered.

'It's all right, darling. I'm here with you.'

'My eyes, Simon. My eyes.'

'You're all right,' he soothed, keeping her hands in a warm grip. 'Quite all right, my dear.'

'But my sight . . . I can't see, Simon.'

'It's only the bandage, darling. You'll be all right.'

'Tell me I won't be blind.'

Simon, with a choked feeling, looked up at the matron who put a warning finger to her lips. So he lied.

'Of course you won't be blind. Now go to sleep, my sweet, and don't worry.'

'Where's Koko?'

'He's all right. I've just been speaking to him.' Sally began to cry.

'If only . . . we hadn't . . . flown . . .'

'Poor darling! It was a rotten shame.'

'Where's Joan?'

Then Joan came forward.

'I'm here, Sally. I'm here, darling.'

'Look after . . . everything . . . for me.'

'Of course I will.

'My luggage . . .'

'I'll see to everything,' Joan interrupted her, 'and we'll get you out of here as soon as possible.'

'I can't bear hospitals,' moaned Sally. 'Promise you'll take me to Great Friars quickly.'

Joan turned to the matron.

'How soon can she be moved?'

'It depends on her condition,' said matron in a low voice. 'She's in an extreme condition of shock at the moment. And she mustn't be moved until she's had another examination.'

Joan turned back to Sally.

'We'll take you home as soon as you're allowed to go, darling. And Simon and I will come and see you first thing tomorrow morning. I'll look in this evening with some of your things. You'd like your own down-pillow and some nighties . . .'

'Don't . . . leave me . . . Simon . . .' came from Sally, who was fast slipping into a state of blurred consciousness.

So he stayed with her there, holding her hand until she slept. Joan waited in the matron's sitting-room with Koko. The boy had pulled himself together. He looked wretched enough to win anybody's sympathy. Joan found herself trying to console him, and help him make his arrangements. He seemed unable to make them for himself. She spoke to his chauffeur who had brought the car from the landing ground and gave him orders, to drive Mr. Dettering straight back to town.

Koko left the hospital reluctantly, anxious to do something for Sally. But he was forced to realise that there was nothing he could do and that he was best out of the way.

Joan saw him off, and promised to telephone him news of Sally's condition in the morning.

Then Simon joined her. Sally was asleep and not likely to wake again this evening. They were going to keep her doped as much as possible. Simon's face looked so grey that Joan insisted on driving his car back to the hotel for him.

He sat beside her, smoking, too staggered by the whole affair to talk much even to Joan. But as they turned into the grounds of the hotel, he laid a hand on her knee and said:

'You're marvellous, as usual. I've never known anybody with such grand poise. I know what you must be feeling inside.'

'It's too awful,' said Joan, 'and one is so helpless.'

'I'm going to meet this fellow, Fisher-West, tomorrow morning after he's seen Sally and I

105

think we'll get Sir Metford Kilwick down from town. He did an operation on my father who was going blind a year or two ago, and saved the old man's sight. I believe in him.'

'There must be a hope,' said Joan.

'There *must* be,' said Simon. 'It's quite unthinkable for Sally to be blind.'

Joan pulled the car up at the hotel entrance. As she did so, she turned and met Simon's gaze. It was brooding, infinitely worried. She knew how worried he was. God, did she not feel the same? So much lay in the balance. Although neither of them spoke about it, each knew what the other was thinking. Thinking that if Sally recovered, they could still take their happiness. And if she did not . . . if she was blind . . . then the last thing Simon could do would be to throw her over . . . just when she needed him most. Simon said:

'Oh, Joan, my darling, we've got to wait.'

'Of course,' she said under her breath.

Then the car was surrounded by a little crowd of people, friends of Sally's, visitors, members of the staff who had heard about the accident. It was a dramatic piece of news to spread . . . Miss Vaughan and the Hon. Keith Dettering, crashing in his plane at Bourne End.

A dozen people questioned Joan. She answered as best she could, then made her way, through the crowd to her office. Miss Anderson, her secretary, went with her. She

106

was a nice girl, and devoted to Joan. She had a strong cup of tea waiting for her.

'Sit down and drink it, Miss Parwood. Poor dear, you look awful. This has been a terrible shock to you and to us all.'

Joan sat in the swivel-chair before her desk and rested her aching head in her hands.

'Light a cigarette for me, Andy, there's a good soul.'

'Is Miss Vaughan really going to be blind?' Miss Anderson asked as she handed her chief the cigarette.

Joan smoked for a moment in silence. She could not blot out from her mind the thought of Sally lying in that bed with her bandaged eyes, and of Simon's eyes, too, tormented with anxiety.

'I honestly don't know, Andy. They say so, but we've got to pray for the best.'

'Why it had to be her and not that Mr. Dettering.'

'He was lucky. Got off with a scratch. It's always the way. These people who drive fast cars and planes and aren't fit to do it!' said Joan, with sudden anger shaking her voice. 'They don't mind risking lives. Anything for a thrill! He'd probably had too many cocktails before he went up.'

'Tch! Tch!' said Miss Anderson, clicking her tongue. 'It's shocking!'

Shocking was the word, thought Joan drearily to herself. As she finished her tea, she saw from the clock on her desk that it was long past six. What an afternoon it had been! Was it only three hours ago that Simon had arrived and sent for her in Sally's sitting-room? It seemed like three years. It seemed that she had never lain in his arms and given him kiss for kiss and been on the very verge of telling Sally that she and Simon loved one another.

Would that story ever now be told?

She dared not think ahead. She told herself that it would be best to concentrate on the present and refuse to allow herself even to contemplate the future.

The next hour was a busy one for her. Miss Anderson tried to take as much work on her shoulders as possible, but Joan was manageress. Only Joan could do certain jobs. Miss Anderson could not take the responsibility. And as luck would have it there were some particularly troublesome visitors. A mistake had been made in one of the bookings. An elderly American and his wife had ordered two rooms and a bath which they had had before, and had arrived to find themselves relegated to others which they did not like. An error made by the secretary. But Joan had to shoulder the blame and the reproaches. The man was willing to take the other rooms but the American lady was wrathful and unbending.

John J. Gander could let himself be mollified because the manageress was young

108

and pretty, but she, Sadie Ganger, wasn't going to take it. For twenty minutes in the office, she belaboured Joan with her tongue, cursing the hotel and its management.

Finally Joan, whose nerves were none too good after the strain of the afternoon, lost her customary patience and tact. She told Mrs. Sadie Ganger, there and then, that if she didn't like to accept the rooms that were ready for her, she could go elsewhere. So Mrs. Gander went elsewhere and took the protesting John J. with her. And Joan, half in tears, reproached herself for not having kept her temper. It wouldn't do to let people leave Great Friars like that!

Simon found her there at her desk wiping her eyes. Never before had he seen the tranquil and capable Joan so overcome by feminine weakness and it went straight to his heart. He put an arm about her shoulders.

'My poor darling, you're just fagged out.'

She looked nervously round the office.

'You mustn't call me that, Simon.'

'I suppose not,' he said gloomily.

'And I'm quite all right,' she added, tilting her head and proudly stuffing her handkerchief back in her bag. 'Just a bit tired and upset. That awful American woman screamed at me for nearly half-an-hour, because she couldn't have the room she wanted.'

'You can't work any more this evening,' said

Simon irritably.

'No, I've finished now.'

'Let me give you a drink.'

'No, I've just had my tea, and I'm going to put some of Sally's things together and take them along to the hospital.'

'I'll drive you. And while you're getting the things together, I'll 'phone through to Father and tell him about Sally.'

Joan nodded.

'Is there anybody else we ought to tell?'

Simon reflected. He had already tried to get in touch with Sally's father who was cruising in his yacht off the coast of Brittany. So far the S.O.S. had not reached him.

'There's Sally's aunt,' he suggested, 'Mrs. Denham.'

'I'll 'phone her for you,' said Joan.

'You have enough to do.'

'So have you,' she said with a faint smile.

'No . . . you leave Mrs. Denham to me. She won't be much use to us, anyhow. She's an invalid and never goes out. But I suppose she ought to be told. She's the only relation Sally's got left on her mother's side.'

'Come down here,' said Simon, 'as soon as you have done the packing.'

She turned to go. He called after her:

'Joan!'

She glanced over her shoulder at him. He looked so harassed and unhappy. On an impulse which she could not restrain she

110

turned back, put both arms around him and gave him a swift little hug.

'Poor darling! Don't worry—at least not more than you can help.'

She gave him no time to respond to that swift embrace. For in a flash she was out of the office, closing the door behind her.

And after that there seemed so many things to be done, she had little time in which to sit down and think about her own personal troubles.

William Hamley met both Joan and Simon as they were putting Sally's suitcases into the car. He had just heard the news and rushed round from the garage.

Gravely he regarded Simon, forgetting in the face of this disaster that he was a personal rival. He said:

'I can't tell you how sorry I am, Mr. Roxley.'

Simon, too, forgot that this young man was Joan's admirer.

'Thanks so much, Hamley,' he said. 'It's a bad business, but we're all hoping for the best.

Ham caught Joan's eye.

'Anything I can do . . . let me know, Joan . . .' He broke off, a trifle embarrassed.

Joan thanked him. A moment later they were driving back to the hospital in silence. Neither of them had very much to say to each other just then. But Joan found herself wondering . . . wondering . . . how it could all end. And what the specialist's verdict on

Sally's eyes would be, tomorrow.

CHAPTER TEN

Joan was never in her life to forget the agony of suspense which she and Simon endured from eleven o'clock that next morning until twelve.

During that hour, Fisher-West, the surgeon at the hospital, and Sir Metford Kilwick from Harley Street, made an examination of Sally Vaughan and remained in consultation together.

Joan felt as though the minutes were hours. She knew that Simon must be feeling the same. They could not even talk together. In the matron's flower-filled sitting-room they tried to pretend that they were reading the magazines which they had been given. But Joan turned over the pages of her journal blindly, taking in nothing that she saw. And Simon soon put down his paper and began to pace restlessly up and down, up and down, smoking one cigarette after another.

The story of Sally's accident was there, in the daily paper which he had flung down. It was a headline story. The accident to the rich Miss Vaughan, who ran the famous hotel near Maidenhead, in the Honourable Keith Dettering's private plane made dramatic reading for the public. There were big photographs of Sally between Koko and Simon. The journalistic pen had put over the sob-stuff with usual exaggeration. It must have made Simon quite sick, Joan thought, to see himself described as *'the handsome and popular Simon Roxley who, with his beautiful blonde fiancée, was a familiar figure in Mayfair circles.'* To which was added, in superlative terms, reminiscences of the gay parties held by the young couple, etc., etc., which could leave little doubt in the mind of the reader that Simon Roxley was like Koko Dettering . . . nothing more than a 'play-boy' in London. The sort of thing that Simon had been trying to get away from for years and which he despised.

Poor Simon! Joan watched him walking up and down with pity in her heart. He must have had a sleepless night, and then what a morning! The telephone did not stop ringing. Sally's father had been found, had cabled frantically for news and was on his way back. The reporters were never off the line or away from the hotel. And Joan had not been able to save him from the publicity and nightmare fuss, because she herself had to attend to her duties at the hotel. Great Friars had to be run, whether its owner was lying in a critical condition or not.

At last Simon stopped pacing the room and flung himself into a chair beside Joan.

'Surely they must be finished now!'

'They'll be here in a minute,' she soothed him. He took out his cigarette case. It was empty. 'Damn!'

She opened her bag, drew out a packet of Virginia cigarettes and handed them to him.

'I'm afraid I've got none of your Turks. Shall I get you some?'

'No, don't leave me, Joan. Give me one of those.'

She lit one and handed it to him. He looked at the tip which was faintly stained with her lip-rouge, then put it into his mouth with a faint smile. 'Thanks for that.'

'Simon, you mustn't work yourself up like this. Keep calm.'

'I don't know how you're able to.'

'You don't know what I'm like inside—I feel absolutely sick.'

'Think, Joan, if they don't give any hope . . . 'I don't want to think.'

'But it's possible . . .' He clenched his hands. His eyes looked desperate.

She leaned forward and put her hand on his knee. 'If the worst happens, Simon, you've got to face it, and so have I.'

He caught the small hand and held it between both his feverishly.

'I couldn't do without you, Joan.'

She did not answer. She dared not. But she knew in her heart he might have to do without her and she without him. Everything depended upon Sally—Sally's condition. It would have been hard enough for Simon to tell her that he no longer wanted to marry her when she was fit and enjoying life. But if her eyes went wrong . . . if she went *blind* . . . he would never be able to desert her. Some men might, but not Simon who had the most kindly and generous nature under the cynical and flippant mask which he presented to the world.

Footsteps sounded in the corridor. Simon dropped Joan's hand and sprang to his feet.

'Courage!' Joan whispered and stood up beside him.

Three people came into the little sitting-room. One, the matron, the other two men Simon and Joan had met an hour ago. The short man with horn-rims was Fisher-West. The tall distinguished man with grey hair, and a yellow rose in his buttonhole, was Sir Metford Kilwick, one of the leading ophthalmic surgeons of the day.

Both men came into the room talking, as is the habit of members of their profession, about something not connected with the case. Golf! Then when the door had closed behind them, Sir Metford addressed Simon.

'Well, my boy. I'm afraid it must have seemed a long wait to you, but we wanted to go into matters pretty thoroughly.'

Simon, pale and set, answered:

'Of course. Well, tell me, please, how is she?'

The surgeon shook his head and put a

compassionate hand on Simon's shoulder. He took it for granted that Simon was very much in love with the girl whom he was to have married in six weeks' time. He did not know Simon well, but he was a great admirer of his father, old Sir George, whose sight he had saved a year ago.

'I wish I could give you a more comforting report, Roxley.'

Joan, listening, watching, felt her heart miss a beat.

She knew before the great man spoke, that his news was bad. Simon said:

'Go on. Tell me. Is she going to be blind?'

Then the answer was given . . . It fell like the knell of doom upon both Simon's and Joan's ears. Doom for poor, wretched Sally. Their own doom.

'Yes,' Metford Kilwick answered in a low, regretful voice. 'I'm afraid she is.'

Simon turned, walked past Joan and stood at the window, staring out. The matron whispered to Joan:

'How dreadful for him, poor boy! Almost as bad as it is for her.'

Joan shook her head helplessly. The effect of the verdict was staggering. She could not really analyse her emotions. Her most vivid sensation was of violent pity for Sally. Sally . . . blind! What a ghastly thought. Ghastly for anybody in the world. Sheer hell for a young and pretty girl who was bubbling over with the joy of life. Poor, *poor* Sally!

And poor Simon! It seemed all the more dreadful to Joan, knowing that he was no longer in love with Sally. None of these other people knew. They had no idea that this time yesterday, Simon had been making up his mind to break his engagement because he loved her, Joan. It was ten thousand pities that those words of love had ever been spoken between them. It seemed to make things so much worse. It was as though the gate of heaven had opened, shown them a glimpse of the paradise which might have been theirs . . . then shut again forever. For, of course, they could never tell Sally now.

All these people were sympathising with Simon, believing that he adored Sally. They were telling him that he, alone, could comfort her and that it would be a consolation to him to know that he was helping her over the bitterness of the blow which had fallen upon her. They didn't know what a frightful effort it would be to him to carry on. Of course he was sorry . . . horribly sorry for Sally. Anybody would be. Anybody would want to be kind and to help her. But he wouldn't want to marry her now any more than he wanted to before. If as much. For what, in God's name, could his life be with a wife who was blind? What would it cost him to bury his real feelings, say good-bye to the woman that he wanted and take on the task of guide and comforter to a girl under the most depressing circumstances?

As for herself . . . Joan could not begin to think how it would affect her personally. She only knew that Metford Kilwick's verdict had crashed all her hopes, and that she must not dwell upon her own particular misery just now. For there was too much to be done for Sally and for Simon. Whatever strength she had, she must muster up now, and lend to them. They would need it. Especially Sally.

Simon turned back from the window to the others. His face looked ashen.

'There isn't any hope?'

The two doctors exchanged glances. Fisher-West spoke this time:

'Sir Metford thinks not. We examined Miss Vaughan's eyes through the thermoscope and there is a condition known as detachment of the retina. In both eyes, unfortunately.'

'And no operation can cure her?' asked Simon.

'If we could have found a hole in the retina it would have been possible, but we could not,' said Sir Metford Kilwick. 'I assure you, we are both of the same opinion. An operation would be quite useless and merely put Miss Vaughan to unnecessary pain and raise her hopes to no purpose.'

Simon stared at both the men. His eyes looked black in his ashen face.

'I can't believe that she can be blinded . . . yet so little hurt in any other way.'

'It was the tremendous shock . . . she apparently fell against her eyes and the jolt detached the retina,' said Metford Kilwick. 'A horrible thing to have happened, my boy . . . but there it is. I only wish I could give you more hope.'

Simon Roxley stood very still. It was not very easy in that hour to sum up the total of his loss. Hope and happiness had gone. That meant Joan would go from him, too. He did not even look at her there in that room full of people. He only knew he wanted to go away from everybody, go somewhere where he could be quiet, and think it all out. Fight it out in his own way.

His duty lay very clear in front of him. He could have thrown Sally over while she was the Sally of former days. A Sally who, with her youth, her beauty, her riches, would never be alone for long. A Sally who was flippant and superficial and who would soon have found another love. That Sally, he could have left for Joan. *Would* have left for Joan. But not this girl who, two specialists were telling him, would never be able to see again. All the brightness had gone out of her life just as it had gone out of her eyes. And he who had taken her love and gifts before, could not reject them now. It was up to him to help her through and make the tragedy seem less, by all the means that were within his power.

He said:

'Thank you. Thank you both for all you have said. And for all you have done. I'll go and see Miss Vaughan now.'

Joan, with agony in her heart, watched him walk across to the door, saw him turn back and look at the doctors.

'When can she be moved?' he asked them. 'I think she's anxious to get home as soon as possible.'

Fisher-West spoke to the specialist for a second, then answered:

'In a day or so, Mr. Roxley. Let her recover from the shock first of all.'

'Right,' said Simon, tersely, and walked out of the room.

Joan gathered up her bag and spoke to the matron. 'I'll get along now, back to the hotel.'

'I expect you've got a lot to do, Miss Parwood,' said the matron kindly.

'Yes. If Miss Vaughan asks for me . . .' then she stopped and bit her lip . . . 'No, I remember now, I can't go, I must wait. Mr. Roxley will want the car.'

'Sit here, my dear, and I'll send you a cup of coffee,' said the matron.

'No, thank you, matron. I couldn't drink anything.'

'Poor child, it's upset you, hasn't it? Miss Vaughan is a great friend of yours.'

'Yes, we were at school together.'

'A dreadful thing for her. Dreadful! I can think of nothing worse than blindness, for one so young.'

Joan felt suddenly quite sick. She turned so white that the matron made her sit down.

'What you need is a stiff drink. I'll ring for one of the nurses to get you a drop of brandy.'

Joan recovered herself.

'I want nothing, really. It's just . . . Oh! It can't be true . . . it can't be true that she'll never see again.' The matron shook her head solemnly.

'It's true enough, my dear. But she'll learn to use her fingers. You'll see. The blind are so wonderful.'

Joan put her face in her hands.

The tears were scorching her eyes. Tears hot with pity for Sally.

'It doesn't seem right. It's wicked! Why should it have happened?'

The matron patted her shoulder.

'You must be brave. She'll want some of your courage to help her, as well as her own. They haven't told her just now. They thought it best not to. She wants to be a bit stronger before she hears.'

Joan lifted a wet face.

'I can't think what she'll do—how she'll take it.'

'And what about that poor young man? They were going to be married quite soon. Weren't they?'

Now a crimson flush stained Joan's cheeks. She put her hands over her eyes again.

'Yes.'

'I expect she'll offer to set him free when she knows she's going to be blind.'

Joan swallowed hard. When she spoke again she did so quite calmly.

'I'm sure Mr. Roxley won't alter his plans because of that.'

But even while she said the words she felt that she had put a knife through her heart.

And while she sat there, waiting for Simon, there were many knives being put into Simon's heart, too.

In Sally's pathetic, bare little room, he sat beside the bed trying to comfort her. Sally did not know the truth but she had a presentiment. Hers was not a strong nature like Joan's. She did not find it easy to endure pain or terror. Frightened, and still suffering from the nervous shock of the crash, she clung on to Simon's hand and whimpered like a scared child.

'They won't tell me when I'll be able to see again. They keep putting me off when I ask questions. I believe something's wrong with my eyes. There must be, Simon. Oh! Simon, when they took the bandages off and made tests, I couldn't see anything. *I couldn't see!*'

'Hush, don't upset yourself like this, Sally darling,' he tried to comfort her. 'You mustn't lose hope. Everything possible is being done.'

The golden head moved from side to side in a tortured way. It wrung Simon's heart to

122

watch her. He could feel greater tenderness for this blinded, helpless girl than he had felt for the Sally who laughed and danced through life. Tenderness but not love. That was the immense pity of it. He carried her small groping hands to his lips and kissed them repeatedly.

'I'm here with you, darling. There's nothing to worry about. I'm here. And I'll always be here when you want me.'

His voice and his strong, warm fingers gave her courage.

'You are sweet to me, Simon.'

A dull red crept up under his tan. He was thankful that she could not see it. But he felt mean and guilty at the thought of what he had meant to say to her yesterday.

Was it only yesterday that he had held Joan close to his heart and told her that he loved her so madly? It seemed like aeons ago. That hour with Joan must have been in another world, not this one in which he was living now. He could do nothing but kiss Sally's hands again and again, and utter words of sympathy and encouragement.

'We'll get you out of here the day after tomorrow. I'll fetch you in the big closed car from the hotel. You shall have a nurse there. Everything will be done for you, darling.'

'I want Joan,' Sally said with a sob.

'She'll be there, of course.'

But he thought:

123

'It'll be too much . . . if I have to see Joan every day and yet keep away from her side. My God, this is all going to be too much for any man!'

'Simon, I want to see Joan,' whimpered Sally.

'I'll send for her, darling.'

A nurse was found and sent to the matron's room to fetch Miss Parwood. Simon went back to Sally's bedside. She was calming down a little. She seemed glad to hear that her father was on his way to her. She was fond of the old man. Glad, too, that Koko had escaped so lightly.

'Poor Koko, Simon. He wrote to me. The nurse read the letter to me this morning. He's so miserable because he feels that he is responsible for the crash.'

Simon scowled at the thought of the wretched Koko.

'He had no damn right to take you up in that damn plane.'

The door opened and Joan came in. For an instant her gaze met Simon's. They looked at each other wretchedly and without hope. Then Joan concentrated on the girl who needed her so badly. She went forward and took one of Sally's hands.

'Hullo, darling, here I am.'

And now Sally clung to Joan, just as she had clung to Simon. Terrified, weeping.

'I'm so frightened, Joan, I can't see. And

124

they won't tell me what's the matter or when I will be able to see again. Joan, I'm not going blind, am I?'

Joan answered quickly because she dared not hesitate:

'Of course you're not. Now Sally, don't be a bad girl. You want as much rest and sleep as you can get. You're to stop worrying about yourself and keep quiet or you'll never get well.'

Sally drew a long sigh.

'Well, as long as there's nothing seriously wrong with my sight I don't care.'

Silence. For an instant Joan and Simon exchanged guilty, miserable glances. Then Joan said with forced gaiety:

'We'll soon get you out of here and back to your lovely bed at Great Friars.'

'They say I shan't have to stay in bed long.'

'Of course you won't.'

'I must get fit. I'm going to be married in six weeks' time.'

Joan hung on to herself desperately, praying that she would not give anything away. She dared not look at Simon.

'Of course, Sally,' she said.

'Simon, you won't want to totter up the aisle with a bride who can't see which way she is going or which man she is marrying?' Sally asked her fiancé with a feeble attempt at humour.

'Oh, we'll totter up deaf, dumb or . . .' He

stopped. He was going to say 'blind'. He couldn't. The word stuck in his throat. He added: 'Or totally incapacitated, my sweet. Now stop worrying, as Joan says and go to sleep.'

At last Sally consented to lie quiet and give herself up to sleep. She was in no pain now. Sir Metford Kilwick had put drops in her eyes which deadened all feeling.

Ten minutes later Joan and Simon found themselves back in the car driving back to Great Friars. They both sat silent for the first few minutes. They were both feeling the same way; completely shaken and as though they had just come through a frightful, buffeting storm. Neither of them took the slightest notice of what was going on around them. The June morning was warm. The sun streamed down from a sky of exquisite blue. A perfect day for the river. And a day black with tragedy for those two driving down the busy main road towards Sally's hotel.

After they had covered about a mile, Simon drew up the big car and switched off the engine.

'I must stop and have a cigarette. I feel absolutely done,' he said.

'So do I,' said Joan.

He lit a cigarette for her and then one for himself. 'When we get back, let's both get tight.'

She gave a laugh which sounded thin and

126

unreal. 'A lot of good that'll do! No, we have got to stay pretty sober and face this thing out.'

'It'll be too awful when she knows the truth. The whole thing's a nightmare.'

'I suppose they'll tell her in a day or two.'

'Yes,' said Joan.

'Joan,' he said and, turning, took her hand in a tight grip, 'what the devil are we going to do about it?'

'Nothing. That's what's so awful. We can't do anything now.'

'You see, don't you, Joan, that I've got to marry her after this?'

'Of course. And for God's sake don't apologise to me.'

'You understand everything as usual. You're so marvellous. And you know how much I love you and how much I wanted you for my wife, Joan.'

Her hand was dry and shaking in his.

'Yes, I know.'

'Oh, Joan, my sweet, my dear, *dearest* Joan!' With a little groan, he flung his cigarette out of the car window and took her in his arms.

'I must hold you for a moment. I must or else go crazy. It's been a ghastly morning, Joan. I think I'd have gone mad if you hadn't been there. It was so awful to watch her like that and know that she'll never see us again.'

Joan put her arms about his neck. Cheek to cheek they rested like derelicts, lost and afraid, flung up on a desert beach, knowing rescue is impossible. With passionate misery they exchanged long, hungry kisses, trying to console and encourage one another.

'It's terrible for you, Simon—to have to go through with it all,' Joan said, forgetting her own misery. 'It's going to be so much worse for you than for me. At least I can be alone.'

He smoothed the dark ruffled hair back from her forehead and pressed long kisses on her eyelids with their lovely curled lashes. He stroked her cheeks and her throat, tracing every feature of her face as though committing each contour to memory.

'I love you with every breath in my body, Joan. I don't know how I'm going to carry on apart from you. It'll be absolute hell, my dear. I envy you your loneliness.'

'But you couldn't let her down, Simon.'

'No. Even if she offers me my freedom I shan't take it:

'That's what I told the matron,' Joan said, almost with pride.

'I'll have to take care of her for the rest of her life, poor child.'

Joan drew away from his arms and gave a long sigh.

'And all I shall have to help me will be my memories and the fact that you meant to break with her and marry me.'

Simon's dark, narrow eyes turned from Joan and stared through the windscreen of the car at the sunlit road. Those eyes were bitter and resentful.

'I don't feel at all in heroic mood, Joan. Apart from my pity for her, I just want to commit murder.'

'Who on, me?' she asked with a wretched laugh.

He turned back to her and buried his face against her neck.

'No, darling lovely one. On everybody else in the world. It's so infernal of fate to have done this to Sally and to us.'

'An ironic jest if it can be called that.'

'God!' he said, 'if only we could wake up and find it wasn't true.'

'I'm afraid it is.'

'Well, whatever you do, don't run away from me yet, Joan. Stay and help me out, my dear. I suppose you'll want to quit Great Friars sooner or later, but for lord's sake don't walk out on me yet.'

She gave another dismal laugh.

'I couldn't if I wanted to, darling. Don't forget I'm just an employee and I've got to give in my notice. I can't give it while my employer's in this critical condition.'

'She's so fond of you. She'll want you when she gets back. And particularly after she knows the worst.'

'I won't go until you . . . until you are married,' said Joan, with difficulty.

Two little white lines showed on either side of Simon's mouth. For an instant he held Joan fiercely to his heart.

'I'll try and be loyal to her, Joan. I'll marry her. I'll do everything on earth for her. But don't take your love away from me yet,' he said in anguish.

She kissed him back, conscious of her own acute aching need of his arms and his lips.

'I'll never stop loving you, Simon. Long after I must stop seeing you, I'll love you. I'll love you for ever, *for ever*, my darling.'

Again and again their lips clung. Then white and shaking, Simon put her away from him, switched on the engine and steered the car down the road.

Joan took a puff out of her bag and, with the help of a mirror, tried to powder her flushed, distraught young face. In a few moments they would be back at Great Friars and she would have to talk business with Miss Anderson, control the staff, give herself up to her duties, But she wondered how she was going to get through the rest of this day. And how Simon would get through. And most of all, how poor Sally would take the terrible blow which must fall upon her when they told her that she was blind.

CHAPTER ELEVEN

They kept the truth from Sally for as long as they could. Fisher-West advised that it would be best for her to get over the immediate shock of the accident before giving her that second and terrible blow.

But she did not have to stay in the hospital for more than forty-eight hours. The cuts and bruises on her forehead and scalp were slight. The worst flesh wounds were over one eyebrow and between the eyes. But these could be dressed by a nurse at home. And it was Sally's wish that she should go back to Great Friars at once.

Her father was nearing England and would be with her tomorrow. She did not want the doting old man to find his cherished 'Babe', as he called her, in a hospital.

'Put lots of lovely flowers in my room and get my bed as near the window as possible so that I can see the river when the bandages are off,' were Sally's orders to Joan.

Joan, her heart heavy as lead, agreed to everything.

But while she and the maid who looked after Miss Vaughan's suite prepared that room, she could hardly restrain her tears.

Poor Sally, who thought that her bandages would be off in a few days' time, and that she would see the river, the flowers and the faces of her friends! And she wouldn't. Poor, luckless Sally, she would never see them again.

Joan worked feverishly to make the room beautiful even though it could not be for Sally's benefit. She almost tried to persuade herself that the specialist's verdict was wrong.

As soon as old Vaughan got here, of course, he would spend half his fortune on oculists; he wouldn't be content with Sir Metford's or Fisher-West's report. Nor with English opticians only. He would get Eye-men over from the Continent. He would do everything, spend anything in order to recover Sally's sight. But Joan knew that there was little hope. Metford Kilwick couldn't be all that wrong.

On the fourth day after the crash at Bourne End, Sally Vaughan was brought back to Great Friars.

They brought her as quietly as possible and without fuss. The reporters had hoped to get some camera-shots, but Joan had lied shamelessly whenever she was questioned, and they never found out when Sally Vaughan left the hospital. The last thing either Joan or Simon wanted was for Sally to be interviewed and questioned and for any tactless remarks to be made which would rouse her suspicions about her sight.

Let her be happy while she could! Let her body get quite strong before they shattered her peace of mind.

Simon, himself, drove Sally's big saloon from Maidenhead to the hotel. Sally sat beside him. A hospital nurse who had come down from a fashionable nursing association in Mayfair, sat at the back. A smart, able girl, thrilled with her patient and the whole case. It was all so much in the limelight.

And Sally was in the limelight, too. Half the staff and the guests in the hotel who knew about the accident, watched her being helped out of the car and brought into the lounge.

Joan was there to receive her. Joan, cheerful now and ready for any emergency. She had done all her weeping in private. But even as she greeted Sally she felt unutterably depressed. It *was* depressing to say the least of it to see Sally walking between Simon and the nurse, an arm held by each, exquisitely turned out as usual, in summer tweeds with a gay handkerchief-scarf about her neck. But there was nothing very jaunty about her head. A scarf concealed the bandages. Little was to be seen of her pretty face except the pert, short nose and the mouth which was rather badly rouged. Sally was so good at her own make-up, but one of the nurses had had to paint that big curved mouth for her today.

And Simon . . . Joan thought how marvellous Simon was. He appeared to be in tremendous form. He was laughing as he guided Sally through the lounge towards the lift.

'You're an old fraud, Sally. I believe you've had a couple and that's what all this groping and stumbling means.'

'You wait till the bandages are off, my boy,' came from Sally. 'I'll have more than a couple. And I'm not going to keep off cocktails now just because my eyes are bad. You can tell Peter to mix me a White Lady and send it up to my room.'

'I'll bring it up for you, darling,' said Joan.

'Hullo, Joan,' Sally greeted her, gaily. 'Isn't it superb, my being back again? They tried to make out I was ill in that darned hospital.'

'You don't seem very ill today,' said Joan.

'I'm quite all right again,' said Sally in high spirits. They led her gently into the lift.

The lift-boy, the porter, the head waiter standing by, exchanged glances, shaking their heads, clicking their tongues. What a tragedy! Everybody knew that the poor young lady was blind. But she, herself, did not know it yet.

The doctor thought it advisable for Sally to go to bed for a few more days once she was at the hotel. She argued about it but finally allowed herself to be undressed by the nurse. Simon waited downstairs in the bar, smoking, drinking, talking gloomily to Peter, the barman.

Joan and the nurse soon had Sally in bed.

That beautiful double-divan with its tall headboard covered in quilted satin of palest peach, and covered with a peach-pink spread

134

of the same rich, shimmering material, had been drawn, at her request, near the window. They described to her what she could not see. The warm June afternoon. The sun filtering through the pale peach net curtaining the casements. The sparkling river. The flowers in the garden. And the masses of flowers in here. Great jugs of blue lupins and all the finest blooms that the head gardener could find in his herbaceous border.

Sally's bedroom was one of the biggest at Great Friars. It had been modernised to suit her tastes. But the walls were as they had always been, with creamy plaster and glossy black old oak beams. The floor was carpeted with golden brown to tone with the oak. On the big dressing-table with its peach pink frills, there were masses of roses, sent down from town by Koko. On the table beside the bed there was an enormous bunch of carnations . . . from Simon. Pale sweet-smelling lilac from Joan. It was all gay and beautiful and as Sally loved it. But she couldn't see. That was what upset Joan. And that drove some of the good spirits out of Sally by the time she had been in bed an hour or so. She began to fret about her eyes.

'I can't go on for ever with the bandages, Joan,' she said pettishly, after lunch, when Joan and Simon were drinking coffee. 'We'll ring up Fisher-West and tell him I want them off. I want to be able to read.'

Joan glanced at Simon. He frowned and stirred his coffee. 'You must be patient, darling,' he said, 'they don't want to take the bandages off yet.'

But Sally was a spoiled child. She was at her worst when she was crossed in anything. A few moments of arguing and she was in a temper. She worked herself into a fever. Simon, Joan, the nurse all tried to quieten her down in vain.

'Send for Fisher-West,' Sally stormed. 'I know there's something funny about this business. I can't keep my darned eyes covered up for the rest of the week. It's ridiculous! If you don't send for him, I'll take the bandages off myself.'

The nurse whispered to Simon.

'Perhaps you had better 'phone for the doctor, Mr. Roxley.'

Simon walked to the door and Joan went with him.

Outside Sally's room they looked at each other hopelessly.

'She'll have to be told,' said Simon, 'that's all.'

'I suppose so. She seems quite fit in other ways.'

Perfectly,' said Simon, with a short laugh. 'She's eaten a large lunch and had two drinks. It takes a lot to get Sally really down.'

'Poor little thing!' said Joan. 'But she's got a knockout blow coming all right.'

Simon looked down at her and sighed

deeply.

'I wish you could take me out on that river in a boat, Joan, and let me lie with my head in your lap and just drift endlessly. I'm so tired. You look tired too.'

'Oh, I'm all right.'

'You're not, dearest . . .' He caught her hand as they walked down the corridor to the lift, but she gently withdrew it.

'Don't Simon, don't make it any harder.'

'Am I never to hold your hand again? Never to kiss you again, Joan, loving you as I do?'

She shook her head, but her eyes brimmed with tears. She tried to do the right thing, but inwardly she felt so very weak, so desperately in need of his hand-clasp, his kisses. These last few days while Sally was in the hospital had been an awful strain. She and Simon had deliberately avoided each other. And when they met, they had been practical, like two ordinary people not in the least in love. Sally had been their foremost thought and consideration. She still was. But it was playing the devil with both of them to sit on their emotions so completely. To put out the fire that had only just been lit. A fire that had once burned so brightly, so intensely for them both!

They reached the lift. Sally pressed the electric button.

'There can't be any half measure for us, can there, Simon?' she said, in a low voice. 'We've either got to desert Sally or stand by her. And

137

as we've decided to do the latter, we'd better do it properly.'

'I wish you were not always so strong-minded,' he said, between his teeth.

Joan gave a little laugh, which had a touch of hysteria in it.

'Perhaps I won't be always. Then we'll both find ourselves in a jam!' she said.

The lift gates opened.

'Let's concentrate on Sally for the moment, anyhow,' said Simon. 'I'll get on to Fisher-West and tell him he had better see Sally.'

Fisher-West came just before four o'clock that afternoon. By that time Sally had worked herself up into an acutely suspicious state. She was feverish, excitable and demanding the truth. She wasn't prepared to believe any longer that her eyes were all right. They had been covered up quite long enough. Now she wanted the bandages off, and wanted some explanation as to why she hadn't been able to see a thing, that morning when Sir Metford Kilwick had tested her.

Fisher-West told Simon it wasn't any good beating about the bush any, longer. It was best for Sally to be told. After all, she had to know some time, and the sooner she got over the first repercussion and resigned herself to her fate, the better.

Fisher-West was a kindly little man and he hated performing his task. But he did it nobly. Holding his patient's hand in his, he quietly but decisively broke the news to her.

'You've got to make up your mind that taking off the bandages won't be any use, my dear. Even when they are off, you will not be able to see. Your eyes were fatally injured in that crash.'

Sally's finger-nails dug into his palm. She gave a low cry.

'Then I *am* going to be blind?'

'I'm afraid you are, my poor child.'

A long silence. Simon was standing on the other side of the bed. Joan at the foot. The nurse in the corner of the room. And not one of them was to forget the terrible scene that followed. Sally temporarily lost her self-control. She went mad with fear, with rage against her misfortune. She stormed at the doctor, screaming that it wasn't true, that it *couldn't* be true, that she wouldn't believe it.

For ten minutes he did his utmost to calm her, but she flung herself wildly on the pillows, sobbing, panting for breath, calling first upon Simon and then on Joan.

'They can't let me be blind! They can't! They *can't!*'

Joan and Simon tried their best to calm her down. She clung to them each in turn, crying furiously. Joan's heart was wrung with compassion even though she wished to God that Sally could have taken it a little better, for Simon's sake. It was awful for him. His face was grey and his forehead wet. They both said everything they could to help her. They would never leave her side. They would do everything for her. She could have her wireless and gramophone. Her friends would visit her, talk to her, keep her from feeling lonely. And then there was her wedding. That wasn't going to be postponed just because of her accident.

Fisher-West made his exit. He left the nurse a hypodermic. He knew Sally would want a strong sedative to quieten her down tonight.

'Tragic thing,' he said to the nurse, as he took his departure. 'But she's a highly neurotic young woman. She ought to have made a better show for her fiancé's sake.'

'Rich and spoiled,' was the nurse's verdict upon Sally.

That was Simon's verdict too. Although he pitied her with every fibre of his being, it was horrible and embarrassing to see anybody go to pieces so unrestrainedly. Finally he asked Joan to leave him alone with Sally. He felt it incumbent upon him to make her feel less desperate, and get her to face her future with more equanimity. He held her shivering form in his arms and tried to sound sincere when he said:

'I love you, Sally. Let my love help you to bear it, darling.'

She continued to shiver and weep.

'I couldn't marry you now, it wouldn't be fair on you.'

'Nonsense,' he said.

'No, you must be free. You must marry someone who can see. You couldn't have a blind wife hanging on your hands.

'Ridiculous,' said Simon, trying to force a note of gaiety into his voice, 'and don't dare try to break our engagement, Miss Vaughan.'

Within himself, he was dying a thousand deaths. Wondering if any man had been called upon to do such a difficult thing. Wondering why he had ever admired or been in the least in love with this girl. Remembered that other girl doing her job in the hotel. Wonderful Joan! How wonderful *she* would have been in such circumstances as these. If the sight had gone from those dark fine eyes of hers, she would still have shown courage and fortitude to the world. But Joan was different. There were no two Joans in the world. And he loved her so profoundly that it was sheer hell to have to keep up a lover-like attitude towards poor blinded Sally.

He tried to forget Joan, and to remember only where his duty lay. To let pity overcome the slight repugnance that he now felt when he had to make love to Sally. How terrible it was that he no longer felt in the least fascinated by Sally's white arms or graceful body; that he could not experience a single thrill at the touch of her lips, or feeling her heart beat so fast under the filmy, chiffon, beribboned jacket which she was wearing. She was not the woman he loved. That woman was Joan, who

141

was much less glamorous a figure, working round the hotel in her overalls. Yet she spelt everything that was glamorous and glorious for him.

'How can you possibly want to marry me?' Sally was moaning.

'Don't you want to marry me, Sally?' he parried.

'Of course. It would be awful if you left me now—but . . .'

'Well, I won't,' he assured her.

'I'll never be able to drive my car again or appreciate the drives that you take me on,' she whimpered. 'I'll never be able to see a theatre or a film or a game of polo, or a race-meeting . . . oh, Simon!'

She began to cry again miserably.

He petted and caressed her.

'Sally, darling, don't take on like this. You mustn't, sweet. There's so much you *can* do. We can still dance together for instance. And I can describe everything to you, when we go for a drive. You can enjoy musical shows, too, and the opera . . .'

'You know I hate opera!' she broke in.

He passed a hand over his forehead wearily. Yes, she wasn't fond of good music. That was her loss. And he could see that there were so many things which she might have appreciated had she had a little more mentality. But she had led a purely frivolous existence up to now. That was what made things doubly difficult.

For she wouldn't be able to be frivolous, now that she was blind.

'Cheer up, darling,' he soothed. 'We'll think of lots of things you *can* do and enjoy. And you can learn to read, you know . . . Braille . . .'

The word stuck in his throat. It was really ghastly to think of Sally's useless white fingers with their blood-red varnished nails hovering over pages of raised lettering. Ghastly to think of her in her blindness at all.

For another half hour he sat there with her in his arms, working frenziedly to console her and take some of the bitterness out of the sting. Once or twice she feebly offered him his freedom but each time he refused it.

'Our marriage is fixed for the first of August and the date remains,' he said. 'I'll get Joan to send out the notices. We'd better not have a big show like we intended. We'll have a quiet wedding at the church down here, eh?'

Sally, exhausted by her outburst, lay quietly against him now. Her hands caressed his hair. She felt suddenly overcome by her tragedy. This darkness . . . this loneliness of the blind . . . it was awful beyond words and not to be borne. But she had to bear it. And it wouldn't be so bad with Simon to hang on to. He was so kind and good to her. And Joan would look after her, too. Joan was so clever and capable. Sally told Simon to tell Joan that she must never leave her.

'I shall rely absolutely on her to do

143

everything in the hotel, and to help to look after me,' Sally said as she grew quieter and began to dwell on her own selfish needs. 'You'll never let Joan leave Great Friars, will you, Simon, whatever happens?'

'Of course not,' he said.

He kissed her and laid her back on her pillows, then rang for the nurse. He was at the end of his tether. He could not keep up this big show of the adoring lover one moment longer, or he would go crazy. He had done his duty. He would go on doing it. And he would marry Sally on August the first. But there were limits to a man's endurance.

The nurse was soon there for Sally to cling to. Ready to comfort her and finally give her the injection which would make her sleep.

Into Joan's office stumbled Simon, looking so drawn and grey that she stopped work at once and ran to his side.

'I'm afraid you've had an awful time, Simon.' He held her by the shoulders and looked with desperate eyes into hers, drinking in the sweetness and strength of her face.

'Joan, it was torture. I had to tell her again and again that I love her and want to marry her. And I did it, Joan. She believes now that I want to marry her. We go through with it on August the first. But Joan, you know that it's you whom I love. You know that, *don't* you?'

She did not thrust him away from her or lecture him now on the right or wrong of it.

144

She had no wish to. She, herself, had suffered torments down here, knowing what he must be going through upstairs. She had been badly shaken by that first terrible scene with Sally. She let Simon hold her close, and said what she could to comfort him.

'I know, darling, I know,' she whispered, 'and I love you too. But you saw how she was. It would kill her if you deserted her now.'

'And it will kill me to desert you, Joan.'

She put his hand against her cheek and then touched it with her lips. 'Oh, Simon, my darling.' He went on:

'She made me promise to ask you to swear that you'll never leave here. After our marriage she wants you to stay and help me to look after her.'

Joan, white and trembling, shook her head.

'She can't ask me to do that. It would be too much.'

'But she does ask you, Joan. She doesn't know about us . . . she'll expect you to stay . . . It's only natural.'

'I couldn't, Simon.'

He drew her closer to him.

'Surely you couldn't leave me, Joan?'

Her eyes, brilliant with misery, looked up into his.

'You can't want me to stay. It would be too great a strain on us both.'

Silence. She moved her head from side to side as though uncertain of herself and her emotions. Then a knock came on the office door and frantically she disengaged herself from Simon's arms.

CHAPTER TWELVE

It was Miss Anderson who came into the office, wanting to know if there was a double room with a bath for two unexpected visitors. Just a mundane piece of business like that to interrupt an emotional crisis. It irritated Simon. In a way it was a relief to Joan. He wanted her to stay on—here at the hotel where she would see him every day, in circumstances such as these. How could he ask her to do so— except for Sally's sake? She could not bring herself to think about it for the moment. She made an effort to still the wild throbbing of her heart—that heart which could never do anything but quicken madly when she was in Simon's arms. She managed to answer Miss Anderson with her usual calm—on the surface, a brisk business-woman.

'Yes. No. 14. Queen Anne suite. Tell them it'll be two guineas a day without food.'

Simon pulled himself together.

'You might go and see Sally later, Joan.'

'Of course,' she said.

He walked out of the office. Miss Anderson passed a quick, half-puzzled look at the young man. Was anything up between those two? She could swear that Miss Parwood's hands were trembling as she opened her ledger.

Of course, Anderson thought, she wouldn't be at all surprised if Mr. Roxley 'was keen' on Joan Parwood. She was so very attractive. And Miss Vaughan, for all her money and looks, must be very trying. Blind too, now, poor thing; bit of a strain for any young man.

'Will you say a word to the couple, Miss Parwood?' she asked.

'Right, Andy, show them in,' said Joan.

She tried to concentrate on the couple who were ushered into her office. Mr. and Mrs. Edward Bretherton. Joan had grown used to interviewing the hotel visitors, and to judging them quickly. One had to be a psychologist; to know a lot about people. These two were young, obviously wealthy. He was a good-looking boy, well groomed in Simon's way. His wife was small and extremely smart with black tailored dress, coffee-coloured ermine cape and a black hat with a coquettish lace veil through which her large blue eyes sparkled and danced. There was an orchid pinned to her furs. She brought a faint odour of expensive perfume into Joan's office. She hardly took her eyes off her husband. And it did not take long for Joan to guess that they were on their honeymoon.

'It must be a really beautiful room,' said the young man gaily.

Joan, tired and depressed though she was, smiled at him.

'It is. One of our oldest and best. Queen Anne is supposed to have slept there. There are lovely tapestries on the wall.'

The girl said:

'Oh, Edward, how lovely! Do you hear that?'

'I do,' said Edward, 'and I may say that a queen will sleep there tonight. The queen of my heart.'

The young bride blushed delightfully, and laughed. Joan turned away. She took a key down from a rack and handed it to the young man.

Will you please sign the register?'

The Brethertons went away to collect their luggage, obviously excited, loving everything. Joan stood looking after them. There was a natural burning resentment in her heart. They were happy those two! She was on top of the world, in love with her Edward. He was in love with her. They were together—married. Life offered them every chance of happiness. Why should things be so marvellous for some, so rotten for others? Why couldn't *she* and Simon have been happy, like the Brethertons? Why must they both face an appalling future without each other? He, sacrificed to Sally. She, alone.

She fought back the wild desire to run to Simon, feel the touch of his hand, and offer her thirsty lips for his kisses. But no, nothing like that! She had to go to the kitchen and see the chef about something. And she must get hold of the maid who looked after the Queen Anne suite, and tell her to pay special attention to the honeymooners. She sent Andy out to pick some roses for them. And after that she must see poor Sally. But fortunately Joan's nerves were not put to any fresh strain. That night, when she reached Sally's room, the nurse told her that the patient had had an injection and was asleep. After that, dinner, and then Joan escaped to her own room. She could not face Simon again. She felt too weak, too unsure of herself. Whatever they both felt, they must do the decent thing . . . they *must*, with Sally blind; incapable of knowing or seeing what they did.

The next few days were much the same as that long and exhausting day had been. And for days after Sally's return to the hotel, life was a kind of nightmare to Joan.

She grew thin and big-eyed. She ate so little that the faithful Andy nagged at her and tried to force her into taking more food. Joan would come into the office to find unexpected glasses of milk and cups of Ovaltine on her desk, which touched her, but which she drank only to please the kindly cashier.

The worst thing of all to Joan was that she had lost interest in the hotel. She continued to do her duties conscientiously. The place was full. The profits were soaring. But she no longer felt the old thrill of pride when they had had a good week. Everything was so changed. Contentment had fled from her. And from poor Sally who lay upstairs day after day, chafing bitterly against her fate. Joan felt that blindness must be intolerable even for a patient, placid being. For an impatient one like Sally, frivolous, loving to rush madly from one cocktail bar to another, it must be death. And poor Sally moaned at times that it was worse than death. She wished she had died in that air-crash. She could not believe that she would never be able to see the world again. No more shows or films or fun like that. Not even the pleasure of choosing a dress or a hat, Everything must be done for her. She must grope her way around the room, with terror in her heart, fearing that she might fall over something or down some steps. She must tap with a stick; like an old, infirm woman, robbed of all the pleasures granted to a young and beautiful girl.

Joan's heart bled for Sally and it bled even more for Simon. Sally did not show up well in her misfortune. She could not resign herself to it. She was like one crazed with rage and grief. And she hung on to her lover now that he had refused his freedom. She was fretful and bored if he was out of the room. During the day when he was up at his job, she grumbled. She refused to appreciate the fact that he was glad

150

to be in a job, and to feel that he was pulling his weight in the world. She would much rather he had done no work, accepted money from her and stayed there at her side, a submissive slave.

Such selfishness and lack of sensitiveness disgusted Joan and, although he was too loyal to admit it, wearied Simon. He did all he could to help liven the hours for his fiancée. And when he was not with her, Joan came to the rescue.

Joan seemed to have a mesmeric effect upon Sally. Something deep and calm in her lent calm to the unfortunate girl. In her more hysterical moments it was only Joan who could deal with her. Sally showed very plainly that she could not do without Joan, indeed she would not! She soon took a dislike to the hospital nurse, who was too bright, and too domineering. She annoyed Sally. Within a few days, the nurse was dismissed. Sally's own personal maid then attended her—washed her and dressed her. And Joan was there in the hotel to be called upon when wanted.

Joan learned to dread the sight of the page coming down to the office to summon her up to Sally's suite. Sally was so hopelessly inconsiderate. When she wanted Joan, she must have her at once, whether it took her away from her job or not. More and more work fell upon the wretched Miss Anderson. And Joan had less and less time to herself. She was always trying to pacify Sally, and to keep her eye on her job at the same time.

Old Mr. Vaughan made matters worse rather than better when he returned from his cruise. He was never a calming influence. In his way he was as spoiled as his daughter. And whilst Joan respected his agony of grief over the accident which had befallen his only child and heiress, she had no patience with his method of showing it. Instead of trying to help Sally to shoulder her burden bravely, he encouraged her to rail against her fate. He upset everybody, including Sally. He wrote abusive letters to the unfortunate Koko, threatening to sue him for damages. Koko came down to the hotel. There was a scene between the three of them which made matters no better and ended in a disagreement between Sally and her father.

Sally was fond of Koko. She bore him no ill-will. He amused her and she wanted him to go on amusing her. She refused to endorse her father's opinion that she had better not see the young, irresponsible fool again. She got her way, as usual, and Koko's friendship, for what it was worth, was maintained.

There were other scenes. Immensely fatiguing for Joan and Simon who had to weigh in in the end, and do their best to restore Sally's peace of mind. Mr. Vaughan railed not only at Koko, but at Fisher-West and even Sir Metford Kilwick. He wouldn't take their word about Sally's sight. He got other medical men down to the hotel. Sally went through more examinations. Passed from hope to despair, time and time again. But none of them could make her see again. Blind she was, and blind she would remain. It was a universal opinion, which in the long run, old Vaughan had to accept.

Through it all Simon kept up his part as the adoring future husband. And every day the wedding grew nearer. The one thing that pleased old Vaughan was Simon's display of loyalty.

'My boy,' he said to Simon on once occasion, 'knowing that you're going to look after my poor Babe makes all the difference to me. She needs you now more than ever.'

Simon agreed. But within himself he did not feel that it was altogether the truth. Before the accident, he had doubted strongly whether he would make Sally happy. He doubted now as much as ever. She still demanded someone who could be amusing. Someone who could make her laugh; who liked smart, quick repartee, risque jokes, a lot of frothy chatter. He was not good at any of these things. And with every nerve in his body crying out aloud for Joan, he found it increasingly difficult to be gay and talkative when he was alone with Sally.

Those were difficult, nerve-racking days for them all. For Sally, in particular, when she first got up, and had to learn to walk; had to make an effort to gain some kind of patience through the hours which were so long and lonely in her blindness.

A week. A fortnight. Three weeks. Then suddenly one morning Joan awoke, to realise that it was the wedding-eve of Sally and Simon.

Joan had really had little time to sit down and brood about her tragedy. The imminence of the marriage came upon her almost as a shock. The past three weeks had been so confused, so rushed, so utterly humourless, and she had had to perform so many distasteful tasks—making preparations for Sally's wedding. Could any woman be asked to do anything more agonising? Buying clothes for Sally's trousseau. Ordering Sally's wedding dress. Making plans for the receptions at the hotel for the relations, and special friends who were asked. And knowing that it was all for Sally's marriage with Simon. With *Simon,* whom she, Joan, loved with all her heart and soul.

She had seen little of him alone. When they did speak, it was without light or laughter. Just a miserable admission from one to another, that they loved each other, but that the marriage with Sally must go through. Simon could not desert her now.

And Joan could not desert Sally either. That was another crucial point. For a long time she had fought against staying on at Great Friars. Shrinking from the torture of seeing the married couple back after their honeymoon. Much as *she* loved the place and loved Simon, she would rather have run away where she could never see him or Sally again. But that was not to be. At the mere mention of her departure, Sally screamed. It was unthinkable that Joan should leave. She could not do without her. No ordinary manager would ever have her interests at heart in the same way. She could trust nobody except Joan now that she was blind and unable to see to things herself. Neither would she do without Joan as a personal friend and comforter, etc., etc.

No! Joan was not allowed to go in peace. And she felt that she had to make the sacrifice and stay. It was all that she could do to help the unfortunate girl.

And now the fateful day which Joan dreaded was within sight. Tomorrow Sally and Simon would stand at the altar and be made man and wife. And after that Joan must feel that Simon belonged irrevocably to someone else.

What Simon was thinking today, Joan could hardly imagine. But she knew that today she must see him, speak to him for more than a few rushed moments, otherwise something within her must break. She could not go on. If it was the last time on earth, she must have him to herself for a little while. Before tomorrow took him away from her for ever.

She saw him for a few moments after

breakfast, when she was on her way through the lounge to Sally's suite. He was so pale, drawn, so thin, it gave her a positive pang to look at him. And there was a lost, hopeless expression in his eyes, when he came face to face with her.

'Is this to be another of those days when you can't spend a moment with me, Joan?' he asked in a low voice.

Her warm brown eyes reproached him.

'You know I'd give you my whole life, if I could.' The red blood sprang to his cheeks. For an instant he pressed her hand.

'Oh, my darling!'

'Tonight,' she whispered, 'after dinner . . . we'll have an hour or two.'

He said, bitterly:

'I think we can steal that without feeling guilty. I'm giving the rest of my life to *her.*'

'Yes, yes, of course. She won't expect you to be with her tonight, and I'll slip away somehow. We'll sit in my little hiding place down there by the stone nymph. I'll meet you there. Say at nine.'

'I shan't live until then,' he said, 'and when it's over I shall die again.'

She turned a little dizzily from his ardent eyes and walked toward the lift. God, but she loved him so! And she, too, would die, after tonight. Die a thousand little deaths in her imagination when those two left the hotel for their honeymoon. And it would be worse for Simon who must play up in his role of devoted husband. It would be a poor honeymoon for him. A blind wife, fretful and *exigeant.* Need for limitless patience and tact on his part. Three weeks of it, in Italy. No use travelling with her. But an American friend of her father's had lent them a villa in Santa Margharita. There, Sally would have lovely surroundings. She could not see, but it would be healing for her in atmosphere. Exquisite weather, so hot that she could lie out in the garden every day. Invigorating air from the sea. Perfume from a million flowers, and oranges and lemons; soft melodious Italian voices to sing to her. It would be romantic. And he could describe it all to her, so that she could *feel* that it was a real romance. Just as a honeymoon should be. Joan tried to stop thinking about that honeymoon.

With Sally she could always feel more resigned to her own misfortunes than when she was away from her. For she was indeed a piteous sight.

Sally never got up until late in the morning. Even in the old days she rose late, but now there was even less incentive for her to conquer her natural laziness. There she sat in the middle of her big luxurious bed, lovely enough, exquisite with a swansdown cape over her filmy nightdress of azure-blue georgette. As blue as her eyes. Those wide eyes which were now so blank, so dreadful in their stony despair. Her golden curls were fresh and crisp, straight from the clever manipulative hands of her maid. Marie was half French, a brisk, gay, kindly woman. Just the person for Sally, for she was willing to stand any amount of abuse in Sally's bad moments and croon, over her in her lavish foreign fashion, which Sally liked.

There were flowers everywhere. Joan could hardly bear the thought that Sally could not see those offerings from her friends and from her own beautiful garden. She could just smell the roses which were beside her bed. When Joan walked into her room this morning, Sally, with finger-tips that had already begun to be extra sensitive, was stroking a creamy satin dress which lay in a nest of tissue paper in a big white box. And Marie was saying:

'Mais oui, Mamselle, it is the loveliest dress that any bride could wear and you will look perfect in it . . .' She saw Joan, and added: 'Is it not so, Mees Parwood?'

Joan, who had ordered that dress and stood as critic on every occasion that it was fitted to Sally's slim figure, tried to conquer the awful feeling that always came over her at the mere thought of all that bridal dress signified.

'Of course!' she said, brightly, 'you'll look angelic, Sally darling.'

'What the hell's the good of that?' Sally asked with a flash of temper and thrust the box away from her, 'I can't even see it.'

'Never mind. Others will see you.'

'But *Monsieur* will see it,' said Marie, 'and that is the *most* important thing.'

'Of course,' repeated Joan, and wondered how she was going to get through today and tomorrow. Sally sighed.

'Oh, well. Come and sit down and talk to me, Joan.'

'Just for a few seconds, darling. It's an awfully busy morning for me, and I've got to go to the church at twelve to see about the decorations.'

'Why don't you drape the place in black?' grumbled Sally; 'it'll be more like a funeral.'

'Nonsense, darling, it's going to be a lovely wedding.'

'With me tripping over my train. I suppose I was a fool to have a bridal gown. I ought to have been married in a suit, only I didn't see why I should be done out of a proper wedding.'

'Quite right. Why should you be?'

'The whole thing's so miserable. I can't bear not seeing my trousseau. I know I shall look a sight, not being able to dress myself.'

'Darling, Marie and I will make you the most beautiful bride in England,' Joan said, taking one of Sally's nervous, fluttering hands in hers and holding it tightly.

Marie retired to the bathroom to wash some silk stockings. As the door closed, Sally began to weep, clinging to her friend.

'It's all so ghastly, Joan. To be blind for my wedding. I just don't know how to stick it.'

There began the usual weary effort on Joan's part to comfort her. Crying bitterly, Sally besought her never to leave her. The old appeal:

'I couldn't do without you, Joan. Nobody could help me as you do.'

And Joan, for the hundreth time, answered: 'I won't leave you, Sally.'

Yet she wondered in her heart whether she was doing the right thing, for Sally did not know what she and Simon felt about each other. When Joan reminded Sally that she would have Simon always with her, Sally seemed only half-hearted about the fact.

'Oh, I know. And it'll be grand to be married to him. But I'm not much good to him now and he might easily get fed up with me. It can't be any fun for either of us, really, now that I'm blind. Besides which, I know Simon. He's moody. He'll get into black moods with me and I shall be irritable with him, and I don't see that it can be a success.'

That made Joan feel sick to the soul. It would have been bad enough to relinquish her heart's love knowing that Sally would thoroughly appreciate what she was getting, and the sacrifice that Simon was making. But for her to take it all in this spirit, doubting on her wedding-eve that her marriage would be a success, seemed a catastrophe. Joan could have shaken Sally. She felt bitterly resentful and envious. For she knew that she would give anything to be in Sally's place. Yes, blind, helpless, and about to become *his* wife, She loved Simon so desperately that she could have found heaven in his arms, even though she were robbed of her sight. Only had she been in Sally's place she would never have allowed him to make the sacrifice.

She did her utmost to bring Sally back to a happy mood. Soon Sally was smiling again and was ready to have her radio turned on, and to be dressed. Simon was coming to take her out in the car to get some fresh air and sunshine. Her last words to Joan were:

'Of course, I'm dying to get married, really. It'll be frightfully exciting!'

Joan went back to her job and tried to stop thinking about the wedding. Little hope when she had to go to the very church in which the couple would be married in order to supervise the floral decorations.

Andy was typing out a list of wedding presents. There was a roomful of them. They both had a host of friends, although, owing to the accident, only a limited number of people had been asked to the reception. Simon's father was arriving from the country this evening. His brother was going to be best man. Sally had wanted Joan to be one of the bridesmaids, but that she had firmly refused to do, giving as an excuse the fact that she could not be spared from her work. So Sally's cousin, Margaret Vaughan, and Diana Carr, an old school friend, were to follow the bride, and Peter Roxley, a small cousin of Simon's was to be the page who would carry her train.

All that day, Joan worked on Sally's and Simon's behalf. Worked at one detail and another until she was dog-tired—so tired that her mind was almost a blank. She wished it could always be so, that she need never come through to the bitter realisation of her own personal loss and pain.

But when night came, her mind was wide awake again, throbbing furiously, like her heart. This was the hour of her farewell to Simon. Tomorrow would not matter. She would be too busy to think tomorrow, but tonight mattered desperately.

She took off her overall, bathed and changed into a dinner-suit, a tight-fitting black satin skirt with a red and gold brocade jumper, which had long tight sleeves. It suited her warm dark beauty. She wanted to look her best. She brushed her dark black sleek hair, until it shone like silk. She sprayed her throat with perfume. She touched her lips with scarlet, her lashes with mascara. She was not sorry that she had grown so thin. Those hollows in her face showed up the high cheek-bones and gave her a haunting, mysterious look. She was no longer Miss Parwood, the capable young woman who ran Great Friars, but an exotic girl with moonlight in her eyes and glamour on her lips, who finally stole down through the garden to her trysting place. There to meet her lover for the last time. The last time, at least, when she could think of him as her lover. After tonight, he would be Sally's husband.

Simon was there, waiting for her beside the stone nymph. Her heart seemed to turn over at the sight of his tall slim figure and dark handsome head. He was smoking but he threw the cigarette away as soon as he saw her. There was no greeting between them. There seemed no need. Wordlessly, he took her in his arms. In the warm summer darkness they merged into one figure. The misery and strain of the past month seemed to fall away from Joan like a cloak as she stood there with her arms about his neck, eyelids shut, her whole soul in the kisses which she gave in return for his. And she knew from the straining passion of his embrace that he, too, had been in torment and in desperate need of this hour, alone with her. Complete restraint had taxed them both severely. Their embrace was endless. His lips sought hers again and again, covering her face and her throat with wild, sweet kisses till at last she felt she was one burning blush, and that the memory of this enchanted hour must assuredly help her over the difficult days, the lonely years ahead.

At last they sat together on the wooden bench, arms still about each other. Then Simon found words to tell her how lovely she was.

'I've never seen you look so beautiful, Joan. Why must you look more beautiful tonight when I am saying goodbye to you? It makes it so much harder.'

She tried to laugh.

'Ought I to have made myself ugly, then, darling?'

'You couldn't if you tried. But tonight there's something unearthly about you. God, but I love you, Joan. You seem part of me. When I give you up tomorrow it'll be like giving up part of myself, so I shall only be half alive in future.'

She put a hand up to his cheek. He turned his lips and pressed them hotly against the palm.

She refused to feel guilty or let any pang of conscience about Sally spoil these moments with him. It was her hour. She need not pity Sally who would have him for the rest of her life. Yet in one way she was sorry for Sally who could never know Simon's love as she knew it.

'You can be sure of one thing, Simon,' she said, 'all my life I shall love you as much as I love you tonight. I shall never care for anyone else in this world.'

'Ah, yes, Joan, you will. You're so young. You're bound to meet somebody and get married one day.'

'Never, never. It's quite unthinkable.'

'But, I don't want you to be lonely and

164

unhappy just because of me, my sweet,' he said miserably.

'If I'm lonely and unhappy, it'll be because I couldn't be otherwise apart from you, darling Simon.'

'Well you know how I feel, too. You know what a mockery tomorrow will be.'

'I know.'

'I only hope to God I'm doing the right thing.'

'You're doing it because you think it's right and so do I. You couldn't desert Sally now.'

'It's too late to draw back, anyhow; This time tomorrow I shall be . . .'

She shivered and put a hand over his mouth. 'Please, please don't talk of *that.*'

His arms tightened about her. He put his lips against her hair and breathed in the scent of it.

'How I shall loathe going away and leaving you behind. You're so little and lovely and yet so strong and brave.'

'I'm not brave. I can hardly bear the idea of seeing the bride and bridegroom off, my dear.'

'What will you do when we've gone?'

'Get on with my job and prepare the bridal suite for Mr. and Mrs. Roxley's return,' she said, then drew away from him suddenly, white and tense.

Simon said under his breath:

'Oh, *hell!*'

'The worst thing of all,' added Joan, 'is

having to stay on here. Live under the same roof as you two. That really is intolerable. If only Sally would let me go . . . but I can't even explain why I want to go.'

'I suppose we'll get used to seeing each other,' said Simon.

'I suppose so.'

He turned to her and caught her back in his arms, 'Joan, I feel so frantic that I'd like to pick you up in my arms and carry you off now. Run away with you somewhere . . . never go through with tomorrow.'

She felt suddenly at the end of her tether. Weak and tired, she burst into tears and lay there against his heart, sobbing. It was awful for Simon to see her then. His Joan, who was so brave, crying. It tore his heart in two. He wondered if any man had ever spent such a wedding-eve as this. Gradually, unhappiness choked them like a fog, killed even their passionate delight in each other. And when Joan's tears were spent, they sat mute and still holding each other's hands like children; lost, and passionless till the time came when they must say good night and goodbye.

Then, for a moment, it was Joan who broke down completely and Simon who had to be strong.

'Let's tell her the truth,' said Joan in sudden madness. 'We can't be expected to go through with this—we *can't*. You mustn't marry her tomorrow, Simon.'

He held her close against him, kissing every part of the tear-stained young face lifted to him so wildly.

'My darling, my sweet, thank God you feel like that. Sometimes I've been afraid of your strength, and wondered if you care as much as I do. But now I know you do. And I feel we ought to tell Sally the truth, too. But if we did, in God's name would we ever be able to take our happiness—and enjoy it?'

The madness passed for Joan. She buried her face in the crook of his arm and stayed there quiet, ashamed while he went on caressing her.

'I know how you feel, sweet,' he added. 'I feel it myself. But we can't let her down—can we?'

'No, of course not. I was crazy. Forget it.'

'I shall never forget anything you have said or done. I shall love you all my life,' was his answer. Joan drew a long shuddering breath.

'I'm almost glad tomorrow's coming,' she whispered. 'Perhaps when the thing's over, it will be better for us. I couldn't bear much more of this.'

'Nor I,' said Simon, bitterly. 'But I don't quite see why my marriage should make us feel any differently.'

'She'll be your wife. You'll have to think of her, only her.'

He made no answer but sat still, smoothing the dark, silky hair back from Joan's forehead.

After a moment she added:

'I won't stay at Great Friars long. I'll wait till Sally's settled down and then somehow or another I'll find an excuse for leaving.'

He took her face into his hands and looked long and deeply into her eyes.

'That will make things both better—and worse,' he said.

Joan managed to drag herself from thoughts of him—to Sally. She had given her her word that she would slip in to see her before she went to bed. Most difficult of all tasks to perform—to talk to Sally of tomorrow and share her excitement and try to be glad and excited with her.

Joan felt that if she had done wrong in loving a man who belonged to somebody else she was paying for it.

CHAPTER THIRTEEN

A wedding under normal conditions will always excite and attract a big crowd, particularly when the bride is young and beautiful and the bridegroom a good-looking man who is heir to a baronetcy. But when the bride has recently been blinded by an air disaster, there must inevitably be an added thrill to the event.

Never had a greater crowd collected both

168

inside the church and out than was there for the wedding of Miss Sally Vaughan and Mr. Simon Roxley.

Women like to weep at weddings. They seem to have an element of sadness, always. And this one was tragic. There was scarcely a dry eye in the church, amongst the feminine congregation, when Sally came up the aisle on her father's arm. Sally, looking lovelier than she would ever look in her life again, all grace and virginal sweetness in that clinging satin robe, her blonde curls misted by the exquisite Limerick lace veil which had been lent by an aunt, a Russian pearl head-dress completing a somewhat theatrical effect. There were real pearls round her throat and one wrist. She carried a sheaf of pink roses and lilac. Her two bridesmaids wore the palest shade of pink and little toques and muffs made of lilac blossom. The page, carrying the bride's long and pearl-embroidered train, wore a lilac-covered satin suit. The church was decorated with lilac and pink roses.

Every detail had been thought out by Joan. It was Joan who had put the finishing touches to the bride's appearance and assured her again and again that she looked beautiful, and that she need not worry.

But Joan, alone, sat in her pew rigid and dried-eyed and did not weep when the beautiful helpless creature was guided to the altar rails by her father.

Her tears were spent. She felt that they had frozen on her lashes when she said goodbye to Simon last night. She felt that something in her heart had frozen too. Yet it was in bitter agony that she watched that ceremony. The congregation pitied Sally. She too, could pity her. But none of them knew how equally to be pitied was that tall young man with the white flower in his button-hole who waited at the altar steps to receive his bride. Joan hardly dared look at Simon. When she once did so, she noticed how calm he was. His face was set and almost as white as the flower he wore. But it was with a queer air of resolution that he took his place at Sally's side. As though he had renounced his own feelings utterly and was prepared now to sacrifice the rest of his life to Sally.

Joan had been asked to sit in one of the front pews with Sally's relations. But on the plea that she must slip out before the ceremony ended in order to see to things at the hotel, she took a seat much farther back.

William Hamley caught sight of her and slipped into the pew at her side. Perhaps he, alone, in the crowd knew the torment which this wedding must be for her. He was immensely sorry for Joan. She came out of a kind of daze of pain, to feel her hand in a strong friendly grip and to hear Ham whispering:

'Buck up, my dear. It'll soon be over.'

She made no answer but gave a slight pressure of her fingers to show her gratitude for his sympathy. Dear old Ham! It couldn't be very pleasant for him to see her suffer like this because of another man.

She tried to shut her ears so that she could hear nothing of what was said at the altar rails, but she heard everything only too plainly. Sally's: 'I will . . .' Simon's grave voice promising to love and cherish her.

'Until death us do part.'

And then something within Joan thawed and she felt an impassioned desire to break down and cry.

Sally and Simon were man and wife. Together until death parted them. It was over. There was nothing more to hope for. She and Simon could never, never be together now.

Sally and Simon, Sir George Roxley, old Vaughan and two of the aunts were moving now towards the vestry to sign the register. In a few moments Simon would lead his bride down the aisle with the triumphant music of a wedding march. But Joan would not wait to see that. Let the others throw their confetti outside the church door. Let the Pressmen rush forward with their cameras. The sun was shining; Sally would feel it on her face, and feel the atmosphere of jubilation and enjoy it all in her way. But Joan wanted to get away from it. She whispered to Ham:

'Let's slip out. I want to go back to the

171

hotel.'

He nodded and they walked together out of the church. He gave her an anxious look. How ill she looked. Such a changed and harassed girl from the old Joan. He could scarcely bear it. Yet she had never looked sweeter. She had bought a new dress for the wedding. Brown and yellow flowered chiffon, long brown suede gloves, a chic little yellow hat with a brown veil, a smart brown fur cape over her shoulders. That was a present from old Vaughan, who was grateful for the care she had lavished on his daughter.

Ham had no great psychology about women, but it only required a little for him to recognise the fact that her new chic clothes meant nothing to her today. She might as well have worn sack-cloth and ashes. She might have been attending a funeral—the funeral of her own hopes, poor Joan!

He began to stammer a few words of sympathy as they approached Great Friars— she cut him short. 'Don't, Ham, please.'

'But Joan, you look so ill. You can't go on like this. What are you going to do?'

'Work,' she said, her lips set, her eyes hardening, 'there's plenty of that.'

'And you're going to stay at the hotel—with them coming back!'

She winced.

'I've got to. For the moment, anyhow. Later we'll see.'

'It must be hell for you,' he said. 'I know what I feel—about you. And now you ought to be sorry for me.'

Her cheeks coloured and she turned to him with a softer expression.

'Dear Ham! I hope to God you don't feel as I do.'

'I admit I haven't had to attend your wedding—yet.'

'You never will,' she said under her breath.

'Oh well, you enter a convent and I'll become a monk,' he said, trying to make her laugh.

That day of torment was not through for Joan yet. Now for the reception! At least she was busy, so busy that she hardly had time to think. The second chef cut his finger badly, making sandwiches. They couldn't stop the bleeding. Joan had to ring up the doctor. She went down to the kitchen to apply a torniquet. The staff on an occasion like this was always helpless. They couldn't stand the sight of blood. Joan had to attend the man alone and unaided, until the doctor came.

By now the bride and bridegroom had returned. In the big dance-room the cake was being cut. Speeches and toasts were made. The Press was gathering 'dope' for a terrific story.

'BLIND SOCIETY BEAUTY WEDS SIMON ROXLEY . . .

173

There would be plenty of that in the papers tomorrow. Columns of it. Photographs of Sally staring out of her great, unseeing eyes. Simon, giving his set smile.

Joan was thankful she missed most of the reception. By the time she had finished with the second chef, her smart wedding clothes were ruined. There was a big stain on the chiffon. She had to take it off. She did so grimly and put on a grey suit and a smock. She didn't want to be one of the wedding guests, nor join in the festivities. She preferred to be just Miss Parwood, running the hotel.

But she was not to be let off. Sally grew restive because Joan was absent. Joan was sent for. The message was brought to her in her office:

'Mrs. Roxley wants you to take a drink with her.'

Joan's hands clenched until the nails hurt her palm. God, how intolerable it was, hearing that name—*Mrs. Roxley.* Somehow she managed to put on a smile, and fight her way through the chattering crowd to Sally's side. It was a festive enough spectacle. Masses of flowers, and long tables laden with food and drink. Champagne flowing. Confetti on the floor. Simon and Sally, hand in hand on the dais where the band usually played, responding to the congratulations. The great cake with its three tiers of frosted sugar and silver bells had been cut. By now Simon was flushed and

174

talkative, smiling as gaily as the rest of them. Miserably Joan looked at him. She could see that he had drunk quite enough. Poor Simon. He needed that drink to help him go through with today.

Joan took a glass of champagne from a waiter, came to Sally's side and said:

'Your health, my dear, and God bless you.' Sally's blue eyes turned in her direction.

'Joaney, where have you been all this time, naughty girl?'

'Seeing to things.'

'Well, give me a kiss, darling. Hasn't it been a thrill? I've hated not seeing anything, but I've heard plenty. Do you see Koko anywhere? I hear he shed a tear at the wedding, poor darling.'

Simon, who had been talking to his brother, turned and met Joan's gaze. The laughter sped from his eyes. They exchanged a long, poignant look. Somehow the sight of her wearing her working clothes, such a lonely, young figure in the fashionable throng, gave him an added pang. He raised his glass:

'Here's to you, Joan.'

'Good luck, Simon,' she managed to smile back. Sally said:

'Give her a kiss, Simon, she's been such a marvellous help.'

Joan drew back, shaking her head dumbly. She couldn't bear that. But Simon had bent down from the platform. She had no choice

175

but to raise her face. He did not kiss her lips but her forehead. He felt her shiver and saw her face go white.

Then without a word, he drank down the rest of his champagne. She drank hers and wished, stupidly, that she could shatter the glass to fragments.

'Isn't it time for me to change, Joan?' asked Sally.

Joan dragged her gaze from the dark, brooding gaze of the man who loved her. She had to keep reminding herself that he was Sally's husband, and this was Sally's wedding.

'Yes, come along up, darling,' she said.

Then came the business of getting Sally out of her bridal gown and into her going-away clothes. A blue dress and coat trimmed with smoke-grey foxes. A blue hat with a chiffon veil, and scarf twisted around Sally's throat. A huge purple orchid on her coat. It made her look very glamorous, and, as usual, a bit theatrical.

There was her cabin-trunk to close and lock. The last few things to be put into her Airways suitcase with its zip-fastener. Everything was labelled for Italy. The bridal pair were motoring to Dover. After the nerve-racking experience in Koko's plane, Sally did not want to fly. She and Simon were staying the night in Dover and crossing to the Continent by boat, first thing in the morning.

While she was being dressed, Sally kept up

a running flow of conversation. She was highly excited and forgetting her blindness, for the moment. She plied Joan with questions about the guests at the wedding. What her friends were wearing. What everybody said about her own looks. How Simon had looked at the altar. And what a thrill it was, she said, to feel that platinum ring on her finger and realise that she was a married woman.

'Are you sure Marie has put my scent spray in my case, Joaney?'

'Yes, dear.'

'Do you think Simon will like that new perfume?'

'Yes.'

'And you're sure my nightie is the right colour? That real peach? And it *is* a good line? I do want to be really lovely for Simon . . .'

Joan thanked God that Sally could not see her face. She felt that it must look grey. Her forehead was damp. All these details were so torturing. She had to force herself to talk brightly. 'You'll look marvellous, Sally, really.'

'I hope I shall enjoy my honeymoon.'

'I hope so, darling.'

'Let's hope Simon doesn't get into one of his grim moods.'

Joan swallowed hard. She longed to say:

'For God's sake be patient with him. Be kind and considerate, Sally. He's going through hell. You don't know . . .'

But she could say nothing of the kind. Only

177

pray that this spoiled child would not tax Simon's powers of endurance too far.

She pressed Sally's gloves and bag into her hand. 'You're ready, darling. Come along down. Come along, Marie!'

Marie was going to Italy with Sally who had to have her own personal maid in attendance. Marie was thrilled at the thought of a few nights in her beloved Paris, *en route.*

Then for the farewells. At last, Joan saw an end to the long, drawn-out agony of this day. One more brief handshake from Simon, one more look from him, then he was in the car beside his bride. Hundreds of people thronged outside in the hotel grounds to throw confetti and wave farewell.

Amidst resounding cheers, the big car glided away into the sunshine and was lost to view around a bend in the drive.

For a long while after the guests dispersed, Joan stood out there, hands in the pockets of her overall, feeling utterly lost and wretched beyond words. Somehow she could visualise every inch of that drive to Dover. Sally's frothy chatter about things that didn't matter at all. Simon having to answer, having to play up to her, be the slave to her every whim.

Yet, would he not find her desirable? She was young and lovely. She would be soft and yielding in his arms tonight, with her seductive chiffons, her scents, and her feminine wiles. He would have to play lover to her. Perhaps he wouldn't find it too hard. In one breath Joan hoped for his sake it would be thus. In the next she was racked with almost ungovernable jealousy. She stamped wildly on her imagination, trying to blot out the memory of the two who had just gone away. She turned back into the hotel, and began to throw herself into the work of dismantling the reception room. She carried heavy plants and trays, dragged big tables and chairs about, and worked with furious energy until her face was grey and her damp clothes clinging to her exhausted body. Then suddenly everything was blotted out. Miss Anderson was sent for in a hurry. Ones of the staff rushed to her with the news that Miss Parwood had fainted.

CHAPTER FOURTEEN

It was the last day of Simon Roxley's honeymoon with Sally.

He had not expected that honeymoon to be a success from his own point of view. But he hoped it would be so for Sally. He had set out with a firm determination not to let her down or allow her to know for an instant that he had made any kind of sacrifice in marrying her.

Being a shallow person with an aptitude for skimming over the surface of things, there was no reason why Sally should probe underneath in this case. At first she had been humble and grateful because he had married her in her blindness, but all too soon she took it for granted and ceased to worry as to what he was missing. As for his love—she naturally knew nothing about Joan—and he hoped she would never know. During these weeks in the beautiful villa which had been lent to them by the sea, he had done his utmost to please her. As far as he knew she was quite unconscious of the effort it had cost him to act as the lover continually as well as the devoted husband.

But, God, what an effort it had been!

On this, their last day abroad, Simon walked through the gardens alone while Sally was resting, feeling that he could not have borne much more of this kind of existence.

Every day, Sally grew more exacting and less patient about her blindness, or with other people who did not do exactly what she wanted. She had changed a lot. She had lost much of her old charm, for charming Sally used to be with her tremendous vitality and almost childish sense of fun. Simon made allowances for her, knowing how hideously difficult it was for her to adjust herself to her physical infirmity. But he was surprised that none of that courage and endurance which is so often given to the blind, came to Sally. And sometimes she was really exasperating. Unless there was somebody else to amuse her, she insisted on him being perpetually with her. She seemed not to understand that a man wishes sometimes to be alone.

Simon was by nature reticent. He had always hated the frivolity of the existence forced upon him by Sally. And now things were worse. Since Sally had gone blind, still less could she bear to be quiet. On rare occasions she was gentle and sweet, happy to sit with him in the sunshine or drive with him up in the cool mountain air. But for the most part, excitement was more necessary to her than ever. She knew some wealthy Italians who had their home in Rapallo. She routed them out almost as soon as she got there, to Santa Margharita. The Italians motored to their villa every other day, and sent their relations and their friends, as well. Strangers were always interested in the beautiful blind girl. Those who did not have to be perpetually with her, pandering to her whims, were ready with fulsome sympathy and flattery. Foreigners were especially good at it. Much of Simon's honeymoon had been spent in somewhat contemptuously watching young Italians sit around Sally expressing superlative sorrow for her tragedy, telling her how beautiful she was, all of which Sally lapped up, as a kitten laps cream.

They had held parties here, plenty of them. How, unutterably tired Simon was of Sally's parties; perpetual drinks, high-pitched laughter, inane conversation. Sally being the centre of attraction in a circle of young men, whilst he was expected to amuse women in whom he had not the slightest interest.

All the time his heart was in England, at Great Friars, with Joan. He would have given half his life for one hour of peace and happiness with her. He hungered for news of her. All he got was a stray sentence in a letter which she wrote to Sally, with news of the hotel. When those letters came—he was now so familiar with her firm, precise handwriting it gave him a positive pang to realise that he could not hear from her himself. He so longed to know whether she was happy—any happier than he was. He hoped so for her sake, for he had never been so unhappy in his life. He could imagine that she would do her best to settle down and face the future. He yearned to see her again. All today there had been a growing excitement in him at the thought that tomorrow they would be flying back; tomorrow night he might be walking in the gardens of Great Friars. Yet not with her, alone. They must avoid that at all costs. And in a way he dreaded the return. It would be so difficult to make just an ordinary friend of Joan. The whole position was intolerable.

He thought how Joan would have loved this place. The garden was ablaze with sweet-scented roses and great glowing carnations. There were many exquisite statues and the grottos which the Italians love, with their tall, graceful cypress trees, stone-paving, flowers and always the golden, flooding sunshine and the incredible blue of the sky.

He seated himself on the balustrade to smoke a cigarette. Two hundred feet below was the sea, that aching blue water of the Mediterranean. Fishing boats with little red sails, were gliding on the water. A cluster of white cottages and peach-tinted villas were veiled in a haze of amber light. From the throat of some peasant girl, drawing water from a well, came the lilting melody of a love song.

This was the land of oranges, of flowers, of song and of dancing. The languorous land of love. The ideal honeymoon retreat. And all its sweetness was as ashes in Simon's mouth. It seemed cruel . . . bitter to know what it might have been here with his beloved Joan in his arms.

So intense was his longing for her today that he could almost feel her cool hands against his aching forehead and see the passionate love which he knew that she bore him, shining in those fine, hazel eyes of hers. He could hear her voice whispering: *'Simon!'*

And closing his eyes, he could almost feel her lips melt under his in that last long kiss which they exchanged when they said goodbye.

With a groan he covered his eyes with his hands and asked himself whether his desire for her would ever grow less and whether all the years stretching ahead . . . years which must be spent with Sally . . . would be as bitter and empty as these weeks of his honeymoon.

He heard a voice calling him: *'M'sieu!'*

He stood up and saw Marie, Sally's maid, running across the terrace towards him. She looked red and angry.

'What is it?' he asked.

She panted: 'I wish to give in my notice, *M'sieu.* I will expect no wages and I will go at once, today.'

Simon's heart sank. He knew what this meant. Another row with Sally. Sally had been impossible with the kindly little maid who had really done her best to satisfy. Nothing Marie ever did was right. Sally was bad tempered with her and inconsiderate. Simon could sympathise with Marie.

'Now, now,' he tried to soothe her, 'what's happened this time, Marie?'

The maid burst into incoherent explanations. Simon gathered that she had forgotten to do something that Sally had asked and Sally had hit her across the cheek. Never, Marie gasped, had she been treated so by any of her ladies. Oh, yes, she knew *Madame* was blind and it was a great misfortune, but she could not strike her servants.

Simon, sick at heart, thoroughly agreed. He was surprised that Sally had lost her temper to such an extent. Undeniably she was growing worse. At times she behaved like an uncontrolled child. But he could not afford to let Marie go. She was so used to Sally's ways, and he did not want to take the journey home without her; nor be left with Italian maids who could not speak English, trying to cope with Sally's packing.

Simon apologised for the blow which had been struck at Marie. Madame was not herself, not very well, he lied. Marie must make allowances. And so on, until Marie was somewhat appeased. And when *M'sieu* asked her as a favour to him to stay on, she completely melted. *M'sieu* was so handsome, so charming. And such a wonderful husband to that cross, difficult young lady. Besides, her romantic heart was touched by the thought that he was so wasted on a blind wife. A woman ought to be able to see and appreciate his looks. *'Tiens!* but he was truly splendid with that deep tan on his face and that black, splendid head of his. Marie consented to remain at Monsieur Roxley's request.

Then Simon went into the villa to deal with Sally. He found her in her big, luxurious room, lying on her bed, crying. She was always crying these days, either with temper or hysterical self-pity. There were moments when Simon wondered how much longer he would be able to play his role of self-effacing guide and companion. He was not an angel. He knew his own restless, difficult nature. He had subdued it more than he had thought possible, already for Sally's sake. But one day he would be driven beyond endurance. Then Sally would guess he was not in love with her at all and life would be hell for them both.

He sat on the bed beside her, took her hand and began to stroke her hair.

'You mustn't upset yourself like this, darling. It's much too hot. And Marie's going to stay. I've dealt with her. Only, my dear, you really must not lose your temper so completely. You only humiliate yourself.'

Sally was cowed for the moment. She was so afraid that her personal maid would leave her to the mercy of the foreign staff. Besides, her fits of temper were generally followed by tears and remorse. She flung herself into Simon's arms and surrendered to the luxury of being petted by him. Creature of moods that she was, she was soon smiling again. She would like to go for a drive, she said. They would drive up to the big luxury hotel in the mountains and have tea and listen to the music. She thanked God that she was going back to Great Friars tomorrow where she could meet all her old friends. This villa was much too secluded and quiet. That was what made her irritable.

Simon listened and said little. He watched her move about the room. She had grown used to walking aided by a little ivory stick, with a carved handle, which he had bought for her in Paris. She was quite clever now at finding her way about without knocking into things and

186

hurting herself which she had done at first. It was always pathetic to see Sally groping. That was what made it so difficult for Simon to be angry with her. And if he pitied himself, he pitied her a hundred times more.

Marie was sent for. Marie, now all smiles again, made up Sally's face in her cunning fashion, dressed her in a white linen suit with a pale blue blouse, and put a big, pale blue hat at a becoming angle on her fair curly head. When she was ready, with pink carnations pinned by a diamond brooch to her lapel, sprayed with scent, carrying white bag and gloves, she was lovely and smiling, eager for her drive. As Simon led her out of the villa to their car, she stopped him and raised her eyes to his; those blank, sightless eyes which roused all his compassion.

'Darling Simon! You're sweet to me and I'm sorry I was such a little beast. I have enjoyed my honeymoon. Haven't you?'

'Of course,' he said, thankful that she could not see his face.

'Not fed up with your blind wife?'

'Of course not.'

'Is she looking very smart? I used to like myself in a white linen suit.'

'You look beautiful . . .' He could say that truthfully even though that blonde beauty had little appeal for him now, when all his senses were stirred by the memory of a pair of dark, brave eyes, and a dark young head.

187

'Give me a nice kiss,' wheedled Sally, now in the best of spirits.

Obediently Simon bent and touched her lips with his. But Sally was anxious for a little more fire than that. She had always liked being kissed and caressed by Simon. And so far as the physical side of their marriage was concerned, she never found Simon demonstrative enough. She liked to be possessive and to be made to feel that she held complete sway over him. When he was in an unloverlike mood, she showed neither tact nor understanding. She would not let Simon go now. She clung on to him.

'Love Sally,' she said in her baby voice. It was a voice which enraged him, but he had never had the heart to tell her so.

He endeavoured to infuse some passion into his kisses. But today he failed completely. During the first week of their honeymoon he had tried with a kind of savage desperation to forget Joan in a wave of sensualism for Sally, who had all the perfection of form and colouring which any man could desire in his wife. But he had too much mentality for that to last. He realised only too soon that no man could be happy with passion alone. It was 'dead sea fruit' when it was not accompanied by a spiritual and mental affection of equal intensity, and he could feel none of that for Sally. He belonged hopelessly and entirely to Joan.

Sally, more intuitive than usual, drew away from her husband's arms and pouted.

'You don't want to kiss me.'

'Of course I do.'

'No you don't. And you didn't last night, either. Are you sick of me already? It's a bit soon. Most women say that a man is soon satiated, but I don't see why you should be. I haven't had as many kisses as all that.'

Simon set his teeth. He hoped to God Sally wasn't going to be too difficult. All day he had been haunted by the memory of Joan and thinking of seeing her tomorrow; he could not lose himself in an excess of passion with Sally today . . . he could not! There were limits to a man's endurance. He tried to make light of the matter. Laughing, he took Sally's arm and led her to the car.

'Don't be a little idiot. Of course I'm not sick of you. But I'm not going to crush your lovely linen suit and kiss all the powder off your face. I want to take a very chic Mrs. Roxley out to tea. Now come along and don't talk nonsense.'

She stopped him again, turning a rather sullen face to his.

'There's something funny about you sometimes, Simon. I don't know what it is, but you seem to go miles away from me. I don't believe you are anywhere near me.'

'I'm very near you . . .' Patiently he bent and touched her lips again.

'No, sometimes you don't seem to love me at all.'

'Rubbish, darling.'

'I daresay I'm a bit of a bore now that I can't see . . .'

'Be quiet! You know perfectly well that's forbidden. You're never allowed to say such things.'

'Well, then, Italy doesn't suit you. You've been frightfully chilly to me these last few days.'

He tried to joke.

'Nobody could be chilly in this atmosphere, darling. It's sweltering. You *are* a foolish child!'

'Well, perhaps you'll be better when we're back in England.'

'I'm all right here.'

'You're not. You don't love me nearly so much.'

Simon's face looked grey under its tan and rather pinched in that strong Italian sunlight. She could not see. He felt that it was as well, but he was infuriated by her possessiveness. He had done his utmost . . . but if only she would leave him alone sometimes . . .

'Why don't you say something?' Sally protested.

'Darling, it's a futile discussion. Why continue it?'

'Well, do you still love me as much as you did?'

'Yes.'

But even as he said the word, a knife went into his heart. He could almost see Joan's little ghost there, reproaching him for the lie. But no, she wouldn't reproach . . . she would endorse it. It was as much her wish as his to try to make Sally happy.

But during a scene of this sort, he wondered not once, but many times, whether this girl he had married was really in love with him, or whether she was not just anxious to enslave and possess him because she was blind and afraid of being left. She had been so much more tolerant when they first became engaged. He thought she would be easy to live with. And she had always been as much amused by other men as by him. She still was. If one of her Italian youths had been here to kiss her hand and fawn over her, she wouldn't have minded whether he, Simon, was a hundred miles away. He began to feel relieved that they would soon be back in England where she could surround herself with her old friends. Then perhaps she would be less exacting with him.

She was saying:

'Do you remember that marvellous night when we arrived here? I wore a white dress and you said I looked like one of the lovely statues in this garden, and you carried me into the villa and described how the servants had covered my bed and pillow with roses. And you said that I was the loveliest flower of all . . .

191

She went on reminding him of the things he had said and done on their first night in Italy. He stood there with that grey look on his face listening, remembering only too well. Yes, it had all been exciting and glamorous and he had been proud and pleased that he had made it so for his bride; and it had all been dope for him. But one came out of the effects of dope . . . back to reality and pain . . . or if one took too much, it could make one sick. Why, why couldn't Sally be contented with what he gave her?

With all his will-power to the fore, he banished the ghost of Joan. He put both arms around his wife and kissed her long and tenderly.

'Now, my foolish one, are you ready for your drive? And are you going to be a good girl and not just a spoiled infant?'

Sally's brow cleared. She was made happy so easily. A little flattery or love-making went a long way. She adored to feel that Simon was at her feet. She said:

'You're a sweet! Now look at my face for me and tell me if it is all right. Or have you kissed all the powder off?'

He opened her white bag, drew out a powder-puff in a chiffon handerchief, shook it as he had seen Marie do so often, and dabbed it on Sally's face.

'I'm becoming a grand make-up man. By the time I've finished with, you, I shall be able to get a job in a film studio. Now, Mrs. Roxley, O.K. for sound. Shoot!'

And he laughed with her as they walked to the car. What had he gained by this disastrous marriage? Only poor, blind Sally for a wife, the money that was behind her and the knowledge that they were going to start repairing Roxley Manor, restoring the glorious place as they had not been able to afford to do before. Young Vivian was at Sandhurst, about to join the Guards. He could afford to do so now. Sally's father had seen to that. He was a hopeless snob. Without any real breeding himself, he liked to feel that his daughter had married into a family where there were such things as titles, an historic English estate, and officers in 'crack regiments'!

The whole thing seemed rather sickening and mercenary and Simon loathed it. But he felt less of a cad today than he used to feel when he had first become engaged to Sally. For now he was giving her something in return. A great many men might not have stood by her in her affliction, and having done so, he must make a good job of it. It might help if he kept telling himself that, he thought.

The afternoon was not a success, except from Sally's point of view. At the big luxury hotel, there was a *thé dansant* on the terrace, under a striped awning. The usual wealthy crowd of bored, blasé American or English tourists, and a sprinkling of Italians, sat round the dance floor at little tables taking tea or iced drinks. An American band played subdued, haunting melodies. A crooner sighed into the microphone. And that was Sally's idea of heaven. She cheered up the moment she came within sound of it and listened to Simon patiently describing the clothes of the other women for her. But he was sick, sick to death of it all. He would so much rather have stayed in the glorious gardens of their villa, or gone down to the sea and walked alone.

Sally's afternoon was made when one of her newfound Italian admirers dropped in for tea, saw her, and asked if he might dance with her.

Simon watched her gliding over the floor with the sleek young man . . . a Count something-or-other. Simon could not even remember his name. Sally looked blissful, her golden head close to the black one. Her blindness had not prevented her dancing, and enjoying it.

Simon smoked and brooded. It was such appalling luck that she had chosen to marry him, or that he had originally chosen her. They could never understand each other. He could never be what she wanted, any more than she could become like Joan. She would have been so much happier with a silly young man like the one dancing with her now . . . or like Koko . . . anybody who was willing to spend money for the sake of spending and pursue pleasure endlessly. But Simon wanted so much more out of life. And Sally was utterly incapable of sensitive understanding.

Sally had chosen to fly home. She had recovered her nerve, she said. And it was very different going up in a private plane with Koko from travelling by Imperial Airways. The weather was perfect at this time of the year, and the short journey so much less tiring than that long one by train and by boat.

During the flight, Sally only had but one topic of conversation. She kept up a ceaseless flow of chatter about the people that she must meet who must come down to Great Friars to amuse her and with whom they must go and spend week-ends.

Simon groaned inwardly. It would be a relief to him to get up to the City to his office. There would be little peace or rest in the evenings with his wife. The names she mentioned were all known to him. He cared for few of her associates and some he actively disliked. The wretched Koko with his inane laugh and drivelling repartee . . . Sally wanted him, of course. Well, he was a decent sort in his way and wanted to amuse Sally and make amends for the accident for which he entirely blamed himself. Daphne Fuller . . . one of Sally's best friends, neurotic, stupid, on the verge of a divorce. Biddy Vanderneame, American, disgustingly rich, crazy about racing-cars and motor-boats, half her time spent in wearing trousers and shocking society by her

195

escapades. Sally found her 'heaps of fun'. Lists of young men, all hangers on, parasites, repellent to Simon. In fact, the only friend that Sally ever produced to meet with his approval, was Joan herself.

And Simon's friends bored Sally. His greatest pal, Jim Fisher, who had been up at Oxford with him, and was a surgeon, now married, with one small daughter, lived in Wimpole Street. Fisher was a brilliant fellow and Simon enjoyed an evening with him more than anybody. He was god-father to the small child, Joanna, and he liked Catherine, Jim's wife. He had spent many week-ends with them at their cottage in Sussex when he was a bachelor. But since his engagement he had only seen them once. Sally and Catherine Fisher had nothing whatsoever in common. Sally was bored by any woman with domestic qualities. Simon, caught up in her set, had drifted away from the Fishers. But he reminded himself that he would go to see Jim and Catherine when he got back. He was badly in need of the calming influence of their happy and well-ordered home.

But for the most part of that journey, there was only one thought in his mind—Joan. In a few hours he would be seeing *Joan.* God! What heaven and hell.

Came the moment when they reached England once more. They landed at Croydon late that fine, warm August day. Sally's car

196

and chauffeur were there to meet them. And then Simon's heart began to beat like that of a school-boy's when returning home for the holidays. He felt an agony of impatience as they drove through the wrought-iron gateways of Great Friars. One name kept reiterating in his brain . . . *Joan* . . . *Joan.* What would she look like? How would she feel about him? What had happened to her during these weeks that he had been abroad? He felt as though he had been away years.

The lovely grounds of the hotel were at their best. The borders flamed with herbaceous flowers. The beds close to the building were vivid with pink and scarlet begonias. Soon it would be September. The Michaelmas daisies would flower, and the days would grow shorter. The lovely misty Autumn would begin. There would be shooting parties down at Roxley Manor. Simon enjoyed shooting with his father. And he felt almost guilty pleasure in the thought that Sally would be bored by it and probably would not want to go with him. Simultaneously he remembered that whenever he left Sally here, he would also leave Joan. That wasn't so pleasant.

Then he saw Joan . . . coming out into the sunset to meet them, followed by porters and page. Joan, already changed for dinner, looking thinner than he remembered her, in a black dinner dress: She was pale and serious, although she had a smile of greeting ready for poor Sally, who could not see that smile. With a pang, Simon noticed the difference in the appearance of the two women. Sally was golden-tanned, bursting with health, all her old vitality regained. Joan had been working hard inside the hotel and had had little time for sunbathing. She was so white and thin, and had an almost fragile look which worried him. When their gaze met, her first smile seemed to quiver and vanish and her large hazel eyes held almost a scared expression. She looked away again at once.

'Hullo, how are you, Simon?' she asked.

'Fine, thanks, how are you?' he replied almost stiffly.

And then she was busy with Marie helping Sally out of the car, leading her into the hotel. Sally chattered hard. How was the hotel going? Who was staying? Was there an amusing crowd? She wouldn't go up to her room. She would go straight to the bar for a drink. And where was Simon . . . Simon must come and have a cocktail. She wasn't a bit tired. And so on . . .

Simon followed, his face set, all his enthusiasm dying down to a dull ache. This was intolerable. To greet Joan like a stranger and to be greeted as such. Not even to shake her hand. Had she made up her mind to ignore him completely? Well, two could play at that game. He would ignore her.

He took a stool at the bar beside his wife

and ordered drinks. Joan tried to get away. Sally wouldn't let her off.

'None of that old trick, rushing away, saying you're busy. She's got to have a drink, hasn't she, Simon? And she must hear all about our honeymoon?'

Simon looked at Joan. She looked back. They might both have been uninterested. He said:

'The honeymoon was grand.'

Not a muscle of her face moved.

'I bet it was!' she said. 'Italy must be gorgeous.'

'Damned dull in the villa, darling,' said Sally, 'but quite fun at other times. We met some amusing people. One divine young man, Count Uselli. He's coming over to England especially to see little Sally.'

Joan raised an eyebrow. So that was the sort of honeymoon it had been. For Sally it had been made 'grand' by an Italian Count rather than by Simon. And what had made it 'grand' for *him?*

The bar filled with people. Jean stayed, obedient to Sally's request, and listened to tales of the trip. And nobody looking at her would have known what was going on inside her mind and her heart.

Whilst Simon and Sally had been abroad, Joan had flung herself into the hotel work, redecorated the lounge, re-covered the chairs, gone through the usual routine with added zeal, and tried desperately to blot out the memory of *him*. It had been a little easier while he was not there. In the depths of her heart she had never stopped loving him or hungering for him, but she had schooled herself to bear the pain, and accept his marriage with some resignation. On the one or two occasions that Ham had taken her out, he had said she was quite like her old self, contented and interested in things. But, of course, Ham was no psychologist and Joan found that most men were big, blundering babies. They were content with what they saw on the surface. It was just as well in her case that Ham had not probed deeper, or he might have discovered all the agony and resentment that was lying there.

However, she had achieved some kind of mental tranquillity and she had hoped that when these two came home from their honeymoon she would be able to meet them without turning a hair. But one sight of Simon had knocked all that on the head. The first look from those sloe-black eyes of his, the first sound of his voice, and all was tumult and unrest within her again. She was still madly in love with him, and she hated every mention of that word—*honeymoon*.

As soon as she could, Joan got away from the bar and Sally's reminiscences. She tried to console herself that Sally was well and happy, and perhaps Simon was happy too. But he didn't look it. He had lost weight . . . just as she had done.

Sally insisted upon her joining them for dinner. It was an ordeal. Simon was polite, but curiously unfriendly in his manner, which he had never been before. She found herself talking almost exclusively to Sally. And feeling ridiculously hurt by Simon's unusual hostility. It was all artificial and unsatisfying. And she began to wish in truth that these two had never come back. She would rather they had stayed away so she could not see them together, know that they were together, or be made to feel that Simon had shut her out into the cold.

With some bitterness she remembered the job she had set herself this morning, of decorating the 'bridal suite' with flowers, had cost her more than an ordinary effort to re-arrange Sally's old rooms for Mr. and Mrs. Roxley.

There were so many things she longed to ask Simon; she wanted so much to know if he had found some kind of happiness in his marriage; what he was feeling; what he was planning for the future? Yet he did not seem inclined to talk to her. She sat there eating her dinner, secretly wounded to the core.

Later she went to her office and shut herself in. Once alone, she sat down at the desk and put her face in her hands. She felt unutterably miserable. Outside, there was the warmth of a starry August night, and in the hotel, a gay crowd. Music and dancing were just about to commence. But Joan knew only the most bitter loneliness and wretchedness of heart.

'I thought I could go through with it, but I don't think I can,' she told herself. 'I think, somehow or other, I shall have to leave here no matter what Sally says, or thinks!'

The door opened. Joan lifted her head. The next moment she was on her feet, all the blood rushing through her body, turning her face crimson. Simon came in and closed the door behind him. Simon, looking his usual elegant self, in his perfectly cut evening clothes, dark hair sleekly brushed, cigar in one hand. The Italian sun had burnt his face to a deep brown. She had never seen him look more attractive. And he was Sally's, Sally's *Sally's.* Torn with jealousy, she kept repeating that fact to herself.

He said:

'I had to come and see you for a moment.'

She gave a shaky laugh.

'Oh? Had you? I didn't think you wanted to see me very much.'

He came nearer and looked at her, searchingly.

'Don't be a fool, Joan . . .' his voice was rough . . . 'there isn't anybody in the world I want to see more.'

That took the wind out of her sails. He had just been putting up a bluff, like herself, had he? He still felt the same about her . . . as she felt about him . . . well, she was fiercely glad.

She put her hands together and burst out: 'I wish you'd never come back. I wish it!'

'I couldn't have stayed away any longer.'

'But there was some peace for me while you were away, but now . . .'

'Peace?' he echoed the word; with a sudden movement he laid his cigar on an ash-tray on her desk, then caught her hands so tightly that she drew a breath of pain.

'Don't, Simon, we mustn't!'

'I know there are dozens of things I mustn't do or say,' he retorted. 'But tonight I hardly care. Peace! My God, I haven't known what it is to feel peace since I said good-bye to you. You haven't known it either, have you? *Have you?* Answer me, Joan.'

She looked up into his eyes. They were so unhappy and so intensely passionate, that she felt her throat constrict. Her defences fell away. She answered:

'No.'

'You still love me?'

'God help me, yes.

'And I still love you. I give you my word that my marriage hasn't altered me in any single respect where you are concerned. I want you to know that in case you've heard otherwise. It may sound disloyal, but I feel I've done enough for *her,* and I do owe some loyalty to the woman I really love.'

Her head tilted back. She shut her eyes

203

because she felt the tears stinging her lids. Supreme happiness enveloped her for a few piercing moments. She could not think of loyalty. She could only be glad, glad, that Simon was unchanged.

'Oh, my darling,' she whispered, under her breath.

She felt his hands draw her closer. She kept her eyelids shut. Just for an instant there was the burning pressure of his lips against her mouth. Then he said:

'This is my real greeting to you. I love you so much. All the time I was out there, I remembered you and wanted you. It's been hell without you, Joan, but I've tried to do my best for Sally.'

Then she drew her hands away and opened her eyes and looked at him.

'Where is Sally?'

'Dancing . . . that's all she ever wants to do, poor, unhappy Sally. Koko came down suddenly. I think she'd rather be with him than with me. He's more her kind. They have some sort of idiotic understanding. They don't use their brains, only their bodies. Oh, God, why didn't she marry him instead of me?'

Joan shook her head dumbly. She was no longer that pale, sedate Joan who had given him such a practical, casual welcome home. She was trembling, glowing from his kiss. But he dared not stay with her a moment longer. The office was far too public a place.

Anybody might come in at any moment. And in any case, Joan and the love of Joan were forbidden.

'You must go, mustn't you?' she said, reading his thoughts.

'Yes. It's too late for regrets. Sally's my wife, and I'll try and remember it.'

'I shan't stay here, Simon. I'm going to tell Sally tomorrow that I've got to go.'

'Yes, do,' he said with that rough note of passion which shook her.

'We can't either of us stand this.'

'We certainly can't . . .'

'I'll say that my health has broken down and that I'm not strong enough to go on with the managing of the hotel.'

'Yes, perhaps that's best.'

They heard voices. Swiftly Simon seized her hands and turned towards her:

'Good night, my sweet. Let me see you for a moment tomorrow.'

She had no time to answer. Andy came in with a ledger in her hand. Simon went out.

And Joan tried to answer some business query in a casual way. She couldn't think straight. She could only remember that heart-shaking moment when she had felt Simon's arms enfold her and the unforgotten ecstasy of his kiss.

CHAPTER FIFTEEN

Joan walked along the first-floor corridor of the hotel to the Roxleys' suite with a fixed determination to hand in her resignation from her job.

It had got to be done. She and Simon had been crazy to imagine that she could ever stay here. No such triangular position could ever be a success and least of all this one. What she was going to say to Sally she hardly knew, but she would not shirk it.

As to her future . . . what did that matter? To love and leave Simon was intolerable. To love him and stay with him here, watching his life with another woman, was even more intolerable.

Presumably she would find another post. She had been manageress here so long that Sally must give her an excellent reference. Then some other hotel would take her on. But there were few like Great Friars. She could not expect to find anything as glamorous, nor to be as content as once she had been in this place. But now contentment was so much a stranger to her, it seemed to matter little what she did or where she was.

But at least it might be easier if she could get right away from Simon and Sally.

But the easy way was not to be Joan's, as

she was to discover when she entered Sally's bedroom.

Sally had danced till late last night. The Hon. Koko was staying in the hotel. Sally had given orders that she should not be disturbed until she rang for Marie. Simon had come down to breakfast and gone up to the City. Joan had not spoken to him but from her office window she had watched him go off in his car.

Now at half-past ten Sally was sitting up in bed behaving like a lunatic. Marie had upset her. Marie had not put Sally's breakfast tray quite securely across the bed and Sally, with one of her groping movements, had caused a collapse of the wicker legs which supported it. Everything had scattered in all directions. Some of the hot coffee had scalded her thigh very slightly—so slightly that there was not even a blister. But it had frightened her and she had turned on the maid, as she had lately begun to do. Joan, aghast, stood in the doorway witness of a scene which made her hot with shame for Sally. She had got into of her uncontrollable tempers. She was screaming invectives at Marie. Grape-fruit, toast, butter, crockery lay in a jumbed mess on the beautiful peach-coloured blankets and embroidered sheets and on the carpet. Marie with a dead-white face was picking up bits of china. As Joan came in, she heard the maid say:

'This finishes it, *Madame*. You hit me in Italy. Now you throw things at me. I go!'

Sally screamed back:

'I couldn't have hit you. I can't see to throw straight. You're nothing but a . . .'

She never uttered the word. Joan had run forward and gripped her arm.

'Sally, quiet! How can you!'

Sally clawed at Joan, and began to cry hysterically.

'Everybody's rotten to me because I can't see. Nobody's nice to me except you, Joan. I wish I were dead!'

Joan could not even be sorry for her. She despised anybody who lacked self-control so completely. She was terse in her treatment of her friend.

'Be quiet at once, Sally,' she said in an undertone. 'How can you behave like this in front of a servant. Pull yourself together, my dear, for goodness sake.'

Sally lay back on her pillows whimpering. Joan, ever practical, ran into the adjoining bathroom for a towel, came back and began to mop up the mess. Marie stood by sullenly.

Said Joan:

'Come along, Marie, help me and don't stand there doing nothing.'

'But I won't be treated like this,' said Marie, indignantly.

'There's no need for you to be. But you don't want to leave the bed like this, do you?'

208

Marie had a wholesome respect for Miss Parwood. She felt that there was more dignity in *Mademoiselle's* little finger than in the whole of Madame Roxley's body. She set to work to help Joan clear up, and this done, she said:

'I wish to leave *Madame's* service, at once.'

Sally lay sulky, speechless, whimpering to herself, a chiffon handkerchief pressed to her eyes. Joan eyed the maid gravely.

'You are quite sure, Marie?'

'Yes, I've been treated badly enough. I don't wish to be *Madame's* slave whom she can hit and bully. I told *Monsieur* so in Italy. Of course, if you want me to remain my month . . .'

'Certainly not,' interrupted Joan, coldly. She never approved of asking favours of a servant who had given notice. 'You shall leave today. I will see that you are paid. You had better go and pack.'

Marie sniffed.

'I'm sure nobody would stand what I've stood. Neither would any gentleman but Monsieur Roxley . . .'

Joan cut short the malicious speech. But as the maid walked out of the room, Joan felt her cheeks burning. Her heart beat rapidly. How horrible this was. So degrading for Sally—and for Simon. How Simon would loathe to feel that he was an object of pity in the servants' hall. It distressed Joan to realise, too, that there must have been scenes like this during the honeymoon. How utterly Sally had changed. Her whole nature seemed to have been warped by her accident

Sally sat up and put out a hand.

'Are you there, Joan?'

'Yes. I had better ring for Doris to bring you some more breakfast.'

'I don't want any now. My head's thick anyhow. Koko and I drank too much champagne last night.'

Joan frowned.

'Why are you behaving like a fool, Sally? I'm talking to you now as my old school-friend, not as my employer.'

Sally proceeded to drag her damp, coffee-stained nightgown over her head, fling the piece of chiffon into the air and demand her dressing-jacket.

Joan found a swansdown cape and put it round the bare white shoulders. Somehow she could hardly bear touching Sally this morning. She had a queer revulsion of feeling. When she remembered that this was Simon's wife . . . that on that pillow beside Sally's, *his* head had lain . . . that through that open door was Simon's dressing room, the most passionate jealousy held her in its grip. She was shaking as she drew back from Sally.

'Why don't you say something?' Sally asked fretfully.

Joan sat on the edge of the bed.

'What is there to say?'

210

'Oh, I know you think I'm awful. And perhaps I shouldn't have lost my temper with Marie. But she annoyed me.'

'Marie was a very good maid, Sally. I shall find you another at once, but she may not be any better, and you have got to learn to control your irritation.'

'It's all very well for you. You've got a nice, placid nature and you're not easily put out. Neither was I until my accident. It's so rotten not being able to see. You don't know . . . none of you know what I go through.'

And then there poured from Sally's lips a long list of grievances. Joan wanted to stuff her fingers in her ears. It positively infuriated her to listen to this woman complain about life when she was Simon's . . . when she had Simon's love and protection . . . and had the right to throw herself into his arms for comfort whenever she felt miserable . . .

God! thought Joan, how willingly would she change places with Sally, give up her sight and know that she was *his.*

Sally had only been married a month and here she was complaining even about Simon. He was irritable sometimes, she said, and cold to her. What did she want, Joan wondered angrily. Incessant worship. Continual pandering to her vanity! Oh yes! Taking every advantage of her affliction, she was quite prepared to make the lives of those around her impossible.

She listened to Sally's endless complaints. Then suddenly Sally's tune changed. She began to flatter Joan fulsomely.

'I honestly think you're the best friend I've got in the world. I couldn't do without you, darling old Joaney. There's something so practical and *safe* about you. I know I'm all right in your hands . . .'

Joan put a hand over her eyes. How Sally talked! And so Sally thought she was 'placid' and that 'she was not easily put out'. How little Sally knew! How could she know about that other Joan . . . that passionate, impulsive, vital Joan, who was far from being controlled when she was in her lover's arms.

Then Joan remembered what she had come here for . . . to hand in her resignation. She clenched her hands and began to talk.

'Sally, you mustn't rely on me too much. I'm not at all sure that I can stay at Great Friars.'

That was a bombshell which Sally did not expect. Her face looked almost comical in its astonishment. Then she clutched at Joan.

'Oh, but you can't mean that. You couldn't! You couldn't leave me now.'

'I don't want to but I—I haven't been well lately.'

'Then you're working too hard. Andy is no good. You must have another assistant.'

'Andy's marvellous, no one could be better.'

'Then you want extra help. I'll get it. I'll pay for another girl.'

Joan swallowed hard. Her hair clung damply to her forehead. The autumn morning was close and airless. But it was not the heat that brought the perspiration to Joan's forehead. It was the conflict of her feelings and her thoughts. It was so terribly difficult to do what she wanted to do. Sally's very devotion to her made things twice as difficult and embarrassing. She said:

'I couldn't do with more help, Sally. It isn't that. I have to keep a personal eye on things'

'Of course, that's what makes the hotel run so well. That's why you are such a marvel,' said Sally. 'You couldn't be replaced. Simon says so. Simon would never let you leave Great Friars, any more than I would.'

Joan, looked at Sally with tormented eyes. She longed to tell the truth; to confess to Sally that she and Simon loved one another and that was why she must go. But that luxury of truth was denied her. She just sat there, hopelessly, wondering what to say next.

'You must have a holiday,' said Sally, 'we can get a temporary manageress until you come back.'

'It isn't that I need a holiday. It's . . . Oh, I don't think this part of England suits my health!' said Joan, desperately.

Then Sally, feeling herself defeated, began to cry.

'You couldn't leave me, Joan. It would be too awful. You must see a specialist at my expense, if you are not well. Or go away. Yes . . . let me send you abroad for a few weeks. I'll pay for everything that you want.'

Joan inwardly prayed for patience. If only Sally *knew*. No holiday would do her any good. It would only make things worse when she came back. She wanted to go away and *never* come back. Oh, damn Sally for crying and starting a scene. And here she was, thrusting her blindness upon her again. It wasn't fair, she moaned, for Joan to go away just when she had lost her sight. Marie was going. It would be awful if Joan wasn't here to train a new maid to her ways, etc., etc. She argued and protested violently and endlessly until Joan was worn down, until she could no longer stand Sally's weeping and Sally's voice beseeching her to stay. She gave in, regardless of her own despair.

'Do stop crying, Sally. It's sweet of you to say that you couldn't possibly do without me. I know you could. No one's indispensable. But if you insist . . .'

'I do. I'd die if you left me now. You're the only person in the world who can make me feel quite secure.'

'Darling, you've got your husband now . . .'

That sent Sally off at a tangent again. Simon was all right when he was in the mood. But he was difficult.

Stray sentences . . . intimate confidences struck Joan like bullets . . . aimed with

214

unconscious but deadly precision at her emotional centre.

'Simon's grand when he feels like kisses . . . Simon can be quite exciting when he wants . . . but sometimes Simon is so chilly and standoffish . . .' and so on until Joan, tortured, stopped her.

'I *must* go down to the office now, Sally. Please forgive me. I'll get Andy to ring up at once about a new maid.'

'Say you're not angry with me any more, Joaney.'

'I've no right to be angry with you,' said Joan, her face livid, her throat hot and dry.

'And say you'll never leave me while I need you, darling.'

The promise was wrung from Joan.

'All right, I'll stay.'

'You're not unhappy about anything, are you?' asked Sally, with genuine concern.

'Simon's nice to you, isn't he? He very rarely mentions you, but I think he admires you very much.'

Joan waited to hear no more. She fled. And as she ran down to the office, wiping her face with her handkerchief, she felt as though she had been through a tornado. She felt buffeted, exhausted. Could anything have been more hateful and impossible? And that spoilt selfish girl had won. Won again because of her blindness. Joan couldn't walk out on Sally because she had a genuine need of her. And to stay meant hell for her . . . and for Simon.

Somehow Joan managed to get through that day's work. She thanked her stars that that fool Koko was in the hotel, and took it upon himself to amuse Sally. He took her on the river in a punt after lunch. Joan saw them go off, Sally trailing her white fingers in the water, laughing gaily, all her troubles forgotten, because Koko was being funny and they had a gramophone in the punt, playing a new popular dance-number.

Bitterly Joan watched that punt out of sight. That was Sally's idea of bliss. That sort of music and Koko's fatuous conversation. It was obvious that she did not really appreciate Simon or his mentality. And their marriage was to be like this for the rest of the time. Poor Simon!

Perhaps the day would come, thought Joan, when she could get away from Great Friars. Until then she must put up with things and so must Simon. God! If only somebody could restore Sally's sight to her.

But what might happen if Sally ever regained her sight, did not bear thinking about.

At six o'clock that evening, Simon drove home from the station and was surprised and enchanted to find Joan, standing in the drive signalling him to stop. He pulled up the car. She opened the door and got in beside him. She wore a camelhair coat over her dinner

216

dress. In the dusk her face looked pinched and exhausted.

'Why, my sweet,' he said, 'what's happened?'

'I wanted to speak to you, Simon, before you see Sally. There was an awful scene this morning.'

'What about?'

She recounted to him rapidly and concisely all that had occurred. The accident of the breakfast tray, Sally's behaviour, Marie's walking out, and the subsequent conversation between Sally and herself.

Simon listened silently. He had taken off his hat. He too, looked exhausted. It had been a hot day in the City, and his heart had not been in his work. For what, after all, had he to work for? Not Joan . . . the wife of his dreams . . . the children he would have liked . . . not even Sally who had more money than he would ever make. Sally who never wished to bear a child.

(It would be cruel to expect her to do so, now that she was blind.) What had he come home to? Only Sally and her *exigeance* and her tantrums.

'So you see,' finished Joan, 'I just can't do what Marie did, and walk out. I wish to God I could. But she makes it impossible.'

'My poor sweet,' said. Simon, 'it's pretty damned hard lines on you.'

'And on you. I shall just make the best of it, for the time being, anyhow.'

217

'So must I. You know, Joan, in a way I dreaded you going. You can do so much more with Sally than I can. It's almost a relief that you're staying. And yet . . . it's the very devil, isn't it, sweet?'

'I think it's quite awful,' she admitted.

'You look worn out.'

She raised her eyes to his.

'You look tired yourself.'

'Much better now that I'm with you.'

'But you can't be with me for long. That's the trouble.'

He put out a hand and took hers. She shivered a little as those fine sensitive forgers closed about her wrist. Oh, those insidious, magnetic hands of Simon's! They had such power to stir all her senses to madness. And Sally had called her 'placid and practical!'

She stammered:

'We must do our best to keep away from each other, Simon.'

His answer was defiant. He suddenly caught her close and murmured:

'I love you tremendously . . . you'll never know how much.'

She gasped.

'Someone from the hotel may see. We must, be discreet . . .'

He drew her yet more passionately close.

'In a moment, I must go in and do my duty. Let me have a second of heaven . . . let me kiss you, my sweet. Let me hear you say that you love me.'

Weakly she surrendered, arms about his throat.

'Simon, I adore you. I always will. But you do belong to her now.'

'By law. But in my heart, I belong to you.'

A little demon of jealousy prompted her to say: 'I am absolutely faithful to you, Simon, but you . . .'

'Well,' he broke in angrily, 'am I any the less faithful because Sally is my wife and . . . I have to . . .'

'Don't, please,' she broke in, 'don't let's discuss it.'

'Then don't remind me of what is not and never will be, infidelity to you.'

His voice was almost fierce. His eyes were black in his white face. She could see how they burnt through the violet autumn dusk inside the car. After the long, tiring day she was emotionally overwrought and she did not know whether she loved or hated him when she thought of all that he shared with Sally, all that was denied *her*.

'What's the matter, Joan? Why are you looking at me like that?' he asked her.

She hung back in his arms.

'Oh, I don't know. It's all so impossible. Please let me out and drive on.'

'What's come over you? Have you suddenly stopped loving me?'

Her eyes flickered.

219

'Oh, you fool, Simon. Can't you see that I love you too much and that I can't stand this sort of thing . . . any more than you can.'

He released her.

'I won't kiss you if you don't want me to.'

That made her furious with him. He was stupid. Just a selfish, possessive male without any understanding of *her* side of things. Yet she longed with every fibre of her being to reach up and pull that sulky, attractive mouth down to hers. Instead, she whispered:

'Good night.'

And the next instant she had flung open the door of the car, jumped out and slammed it. With her hands in the pockets of her coat, she started to run across the lawn. Simon, his face set and miserable, switched on the engine and drove up to the hotel.

CHAPTER SIXTEEN

For Joan, that autumn was a long drawn-out agony. Every day there seemed to be some painful incident either with Simon or Sally—or with both. And every other day a repetition of the pain.

There were no limits to Sally's demands upon Joan, and she did what she could because no matter how tiresome or selfish Sally was, Joan could never withstand the thought of her blindness. In those days much was forgiven Sally because of those sightless eyes of hers.

Simon was less demanding, but Joan knew in her heart how he felt about things. They stopped discussing the situation. They had both reached the conclusion that such discussions were fruitless and unhappy. But they had to see each other. They couldn't escape that, and although Simon set a seal upon his lips and his passionate desire for Joan, she could feel the undercurrent of it eating her up as it was eating him. It was unspoken, unbearable hunger between them. Joan suffered for herself and even more for him, hating the bitterness in his eyes. He seemed to grow older in a few weeks. There was nothing left in him of the gay boy. He was utterly at the mercy of Sally and her blindness, and at times Joan could hardly tolerate things for him. When Sally was peevish, nagging, exacting, Joan yearned to drag Simon from Sally, and say:

'You can't go on like this. Neither can I. Take me away somewhere. Let's find our heaven, somehow, out of this hell!'

But she always managed to run away before such mad words came from her lips, and, in her lonely hours, build up a fresh reserve of strength to get through the difficult days.

Ham was, as ever, a loyal good friend to Joan. He said nothing more about Simon, but she knew that he was not ignorant of the state of affairs, and he was especially kind and thoughtful. It was one evening after Joan had been out with him to a cinema in Maidenhead, that she had one of her worst moments with Simon.

Sally, had gone to bed early with a headache. Simon, who had been away that weekend shooting with his father, returned to Great Friars, longing to see Joan. Andy had told him that it was Joan's half holiday, and that she was at the pictures with Ham. When Joan returned at eleven o'clock, she saw a light on in her office. She found Simon sitting on her desk. He was finishing a whisky-and-soda. There were innumerable cigarette ends in the ashtray before him.

Joan looked at him amazed. He got up as she came in, and smiled at her in a way she had never seen him smile before. It was a cold, almost bitter smile.

'Had a good time?' he asked her.

Bewildered, she took off her coat and hat and flung them on to a chair. As she did so, she had an uneasy feeling that Simon had had one whisky too many. He spoke to her in a rather careful, drawling voice.

She answered quietly:

'Yes, thank you, Simon. It wasn't a bad film.'

'And Mr. Hamley—I hope he wasn't a bad companion?'

She changed colour and drew nearer to him.

She looked up at him with steady gaze.

'What's the matter, Simon?'

He gave a short laugh and stubbed his cigarette in the ash-tray.

'You may well ask.'

Her heart began to beat uncomfortably fast. 'Is Sally . . .?'

'No,' he cut in, 'it's nothing to do with Sally. She's fine. We danced until she went to bed. That's what she makes me do, dance—dance! Yes, I've been the big dancing partner while you were at the pictures with your very attentive friend!'

Joan, one hand against her breast, continued for a moment to look up at Simon without speaking. She knew what was the matter now. Simon was jealous. Poor unhappy Simon—jealous of Ham! He had no right to be, but he was. And because she loved him with all her heart, she gloried in his jealousy. Yet it tortured her. She could do nothing about it—no more than he could do, when everything in her seemed to break each time she pictured Sally in his arms.

At last she said:

'You shouldn't be in here at this hour, my dear. What will people think?'

He spread out his hand with a deprecating gesture.

'What the hell do I care? And why shouldn't I be in your office? I can't take you to the pictures like William Hamley. If I did, that would make people talk even more, wouldn't it? Besides, if I asked you, you wouldn't go, would you?'

He was white and furious, and she pitied him as she pitied herself, and could not help him because she, herself, needed help. It was all getting too much for her, and for him!

His dark, bitter gaze took in every detail of her appearance. She was wearing a new dress which he had not seen before. Some dark green wool material which suited her. He looked at her ruffled hair, her ungloved hands, and insensate rage engulfed him at the vision of her sitting in that cinema with Hamley. He said between his teeth

'And did your young hero hold your hand—tightly when there was a love scene in the picture—then *more* tightly! And did that hand creep up to your hair and did you feel lonely and unsatisfied and glad of his caresses? Oh, why not? He has the right to do these things, and I haven't. I haven't the right to stand here in your office and talk to you because office hours are over, and my wife's upstairs waiting for me to go up and tell her that I couldn't live without her. *God!*'

'For heaven's sake be quiet!' Joan interrupted, her face flaming, her whole body beginning to tremble. 'You're mad to say things like this to me. It isn't fair.'

'And is it fair that you and Hamley . . .'

She broke in again:

'Stop it, Simon! You've no right to presume that I would allow Ham to make love to me in a cinema, or anywhere else.'

'Didn't he?'

'No, he did not. I tell you, you're mad, Simon, or you've had too much to drink.'

He flicked his thumb-nail against the empty glass on the desk, and laughed.

'If I'm drinking, my dear, it's to drown my sorrows. If I'm mad, it's because I don't feel that I can stand many more weeks of this living death.'

She felt distracted, helpless against the rising tide of emotion within her.

'Oh, Simon! Simon!' she whispered.

Then he caught her close with a savage movement, passed a hand over her flushed face, and up to her hair. She could feel his fingers hot, dry, shaking.

'Don't you realise,' he said, 'that I'm crazy with love for you, that I can't tolerate the idea of another man being out with you, alone.'

Something within her seemed to snap. She could no longer fight him because she was defeated. She surrendered to his embrace, clinging to him like a drowning woman.

'I feel that way too. I'm jealous of *her* . . . of every kiss you give her . . . even though I know you don't love her any more than I love Ham. Yes, I'm jealous too. Simon, Simon, I love you so.'

It was a moment of blinding madness which

shattered them both, left them reckless of the fact that someone might come into that office, even at this hour. Some of the guests were still up. But they belonged only to each other for those breathless moments while they kissed . . . and kissed again . . . in a white-hot fervour of desire.

Simon was the first to recover sanity and come back to earth. He drew away from Joan's lips and from her arms.

'Forgive me. Forgive me, Joan . . .'

He could say no more. Sitting down on the edge of the desk, he put his head between his hands. She, her eyes brilliant in a face that was now as white as milk, looked at him and sought to restore her own balance.

'What have I to forgive?' she whispered.

'I shouldn't have kissed you like that.'

She tried to laugh.

'I kissed you, too. What's the use of regretting it?'

He raised his head and, for the first time, his face relaxed into a smile which made him extraordinarily young and appealing to her.

'No use at all. As long as I live, I shall want to kiss you that way, and I'm not going to deny it.'

'Oh, darling, darling!' said Joan, miserably. Then, woman-like, searching in her bag for mirror, powder-puff and comb to restore her face and hair. He lit a cigarette and watched her.

'I think you're the most wonderful person in the world,' he said.

'I'm just a fool, really, Simon.'

'We're both fools, my sweet. Fools not to cut and run together this very night, but we won't, because—well, because we're fools—about Sally.'

'Sally depends on us both more and more,' said Joan, in a low voice, 'that's the devil of it. But I'm not going on like this, Simon, I'm going to tell her that I want to leave.'

He shook his head.

'We say that every time, and then when you tell her there's a scene.'

Joan, hair straight, nose powdered, and blood cooling down, thrust out her chin in a determined way.

'Well, we can't go on like this. It'll kill us both. I think I'd better tell her the truth. I think I'd better say: "I'm sorry, Sally, but I'm in love with your husband, so I've got to leave Great Friars".'

Again Simon shook his head.

'My dear, that wouldn't work. Sally has no mercy on others. And she's so selfish that she'd waive your love for me if you told her about it. She'd even be casual enough to tell you to stay where you are and go on being in love.'

'She wouldn't say that if she knew how *you* felt about *me!*'

'Sometimes I even wonder that,' he said, gloomily. 'I don't think I really satisfy Sally. I think she's disappointed in me. She's much merrier and brighter when that fool Koko is around.'

'All the same,' said Joan, 'she'd be fiendishly jealous if she thought that *your* affections had changed.'

'So what, my dear?'

She turned away, shrugging her shoulders helplessly.

'So nothing. I suppose. We just carry on and make ourselves and each other miserable.'

He got up, came towards her and took both her hands in his.

'Forgive me if I make you miserable, my darling. I know I'm a brute at times. I get irritable because I'm so damned jealous.'

'You needn't be,' she said wearily.

He sighed heavily.

'I suppose when it turns a bit colder, Sally will want to go back to town.'

She gave him a wistful look.

'Do you think it will be any easier for you to be away from me, Simon?'

'Oh, in a way, I suppose. It's the very devil living under the same roof, isn't it?'

She nodded.

'The very devil!'

He leaned forward and kissed her on the forehead, gently tenderly.

'I'll try not to go crazy again. You look very tired, my poor sweet. Good night! Go to bed!'

'I'll come in a moment. I just want to look

228

up something in a ledger.'

He dropped her hands, turned and walked out of the office. She followed the tall figure with a look almost of despair in her eyes. It was all she could do to prevent herself from calling him back. The woman in her clamoured for his embrace, for more and more of those burning kisses, those rapturous caresses of a few moments ago.

Sitting down at her desk, she put her face in her hands. She thought. 'He said it would be easier for him—and for me—if we weren't under the same roof. It might even be easier if I were not free. If he didn't know, if he left Sally, he could come to me, and find me, waiting. It might solve the problem for us all if I gave away my freedom. If, for instance, I got married. *To Ham.*'

And that thought having once crept into Joan's mind stayed there. It was there the next time that he came into the hotel to see her, and the next. He was still obviously very much in love with her. Not that he ever pestered her with his attentions, but he gave her the friendship which she needed and let her feel the undercurrent of that other emotion which she always bred in him. She knew that he wanted to many her and that she had only to say the word.

And now, every time she saw Ham, the idea of marrying him crept back to her. Wouldn't it be better to do it—and so finish things for ever with Simon? It might hurt him desperately to begin with. But soon he would recover from the blow and realise it was for the best. She would be permanently removed from him. There would be no more of this racking hunger and despair. As for herself, she hardly dared contemplate marriage with anyone but Simon—not even Ham who was so kind, so charming and whom she looked upon as one of her greatest friends.

She belonged utterly to Simon. She always would. How then could it be fair for her to marry another man? How could it be fair to Ham? Well, only he could answer that. She would have to tell him the truth and if he still wanted her, well, there it was!

Autumn drifted into the first sharp frost of winter, and a piercing wind tore the dying leaves from the trees, and swept the petals from the last remaining dahlias and chrysanthemums, before Joan reached any kind of decision about her life.

It would all have been so different had Sally not been blind. But Sally needed her here, and she could not leave her. She had made various feeble attempts to get away and each one met with demonstrations of such woe, such resentment from Sally, that Joan had not the heart to walk out on her. But if she was helping Sally, she felt that she was hurting Simon unnecessarily. They met continually. Sometimes with Sally, sometimes in crowds, sometimes alone. And when alone, the old love-hunger always consumed them and drove them into each other's arms, only to end in apologies from him and tears from her. They had no right to love. Yet how could they stamp it out. Gradually the idea of marrying William Hamley ceased to be just an idle fancy to be toyed with and became an obsession with Joan. She could marry him and still stay here and manage the hotel. Still be with Sally, when she wanted her. But she would no longer be Miss Parwood, free, accessible. She would be Ham's wife, living out of the hotel. When her duties were finished, she would go back to his house which adjoined the garages. Not a bad little house; Victorian, grey-stone, well-built, with a small garden. There would be none of the luxuries of Great Friars there. But Ham was not poor. He could make her comfortable. Anyhow, material things had ceased to matter much. She wanted nothing but peace of mind, and she believed that it could only be gained through marriage—with Ham.

In the first week in November, a Hunt Ball was held at Great Friars. That entailed a tremendous lot of extra work for Joan. She was tired out the day before the dance took place, and on the Saturday night of the actual affair, her one ambition was to go to her room, and to bed.

But it was not possible. When there was a big affair in the hotel like this, Miss Parwood had to be very much to the fore. And Sally wanted her. Sally had asked a party (including Koko) down from London. Sally had to be dressed and looked over by Joan before she would go downstairs. The maid who had taken Marie's place was good, but Sally trusted only Joan, so far as her appearance was concerned. It was always Joan who bought her dresses for her, and who gave the final touches to her toilette. And Joan had to be somewhere about during the evening so that Sally could call her and say: *Am I all right? Is my hair O.K.? Will you powder my nose for me?*

Such piteous appeals Joan could never resist. So, tonight, before the Ball commenced, Joan was there in Sally's room, making sure that everything was perfect.

Sally had been bought a new dress for the occasion. White, thick crepe, perfectly tailored. She wore with it a short white ermine cape, and camellias in her golden hair. She looked enchanting. Even the stony stare of those big blue eyes could not destroy her beauty. Joan, unusually tired and dispirited, looked at her tonight and thought how odd it was that Simon was no longer stirred to an extra pulsebeat by this lovely wife of his. He had told her so only the other night. It was her, Joan, whom he desired, and her alone. How curious that seemed! Joan gazed at herself in Sally's mirror and felt that she was haggard and plain—that the last few months had put

232

years on her—lines under eyes and about her lips.

But Simon Bexley did not think so when he came into his wife's room and saw the two girls standing there together. His gaze passed straight from Sally's glowing figure to Joan's, stayed with her. Joan looked tired, pale, certainly, yet to him immeasurably more beautiful than his wife. A little grey ghost of a girl in a pearl-grey chiffon dress, with a coral velvet bolero, and some coral-coloured roses against her shoulder. He adored that resolute, strong young face of hers; that fine forehead from which the dark hair rippled back like black silk and curled softly behind each ear; those large hazel eyes; that red patient mouth which he had so often kissed in the burning passion of a mad hour.

Their gaze met; for a moment there was a tense silence in Sally's room. Then Simon said:

'How nice you two are-looking!'

'I wish you wouldn't creep in like that and startle me,' said Sally in a fractious voice.

Joan turned away, her cheeks reddening. She always loathed to hear Sally nag her husband.

'Sorry. I didn't mean to "creep"', he said.

Sally took no further notice of him.

'Has Koko come yet, Joan?' was her next question.

'Yes. He's in the bar,' said Joan.

Simon, hands in his pockets, face moody,

233

muttered under his breath:

'Very suitable place.'

A flush of anger mounted Sally's cheeks.

'Oh, I know you don't think much of Koko!' she said, 'but he's nicer to me than anybody else.'

'So he damned well ought to be. What he did for you at Cockmarsh wasn't so hot . . .' began Simon.

Sally interrupted:

'You needn't fling that at him. It was an accident.'

'Following one over the odd, methinks.'

'Well, it's for me to be spiteful, not you. I'm the one who lost my sight,' came from Sally with hot petulance, 'and you needn't pretend you care so much whether I can see or whether I can't. You don't care a damn about me these days.'

Simon flushed darkly.

'How can you say that . . .'

He stopped, his lips working. Joan stepped forward. She was shocked and distressed by this sudden scene between husband and wife. Sally had no right to bait Simon like that. She had no justifiable cause. Simon never neglected her, *never,* whatever he felt. He had been marvellous, devoted, patient even when *he* was tried beyond endurance. It was all very well for Keith Dettering to come down here at intervals and be charming and amusing. He did not have to cope with Sally in her worst

234

hours.

'Sally, *darling!*' Joan reproached her, laying a hand on her arm, 'Why should you feel like this? You know how terribly concerned we all are about you and . . .'

She stopped. Sally had flung off that friendly hand. The first hostile gesture she had ever shown Joan. She was in a white-hot temper now, without really knowing why she was so angry. These sudden, ungovernable fits of temper had been seizing her lately without cause.

'Oh, leave me alone, Joan,' she exclaimed, then called her maid to lead her downstairs.

Simon and Joan were left alone. Simon looked around his wife's disordered bedroom. The air was so heavily perfumed that it made him feel sick. The central heating and a big electric-fire were full on. He marched to the window, flung it open and let in a wave of cold, frosty air which sent a shiver through Joan. Anxiously she looked at him.

'Simon, my dear, don't let it upset you. You know Sally doesn't mean half she says.'

He swung round and faced her. The expression in his eyes was not good to see. It was as though the worst and best were warring in the man's very soul.

'You can make allowances for her,' he said harshly, 'and I suppose I can, when I remember her blindness. But she's become a bully and a nagger and I'm not the sort of

235

person to accept either bullying or nagging with angelic patience. I'm not an angel, as well you know. The whole thing's getting me down, Joan, and I don't mind admitting it.'

She made a gesture of despair.

'It's this triangle, Simon. It's no good to any of us. You and Sally would be far better off without me.'

'What do you suggest?' he asked with a short laugh. 'Taking Koko off on a world tour and leaving Sally and me to console each other?'

She flushed.

'Why be sarcastic with me?'

Then his gaze travelled over her in a way that sent her blood flaming through her body.

'You're looking so lovely tonight, my sweet, that I assure you I'd rather adore than sneer at you.'

She knew then that it would be well if she got out of this room quickly. This was no time and no place for a personal scene with Simon.

She would have given anything to fling herself straight into his arms. Instead of which, she turned and ran from Sally's bedroom, down the stairs and into the lounge, where there were crowds, bright lights, music. A gay and festive atmosphere. Things for her to do. Anything rather than be alone with Simon in his devil's mood, knowing how much she wanted to forget Sally and give herself utterly to love and her lover.

She saw Ham's tall figure moving through the lounge towards her. Ham; a little red and self-conscious in his tails. He hated them. He was like a schoolboy, never at home in such clothes. He so much preferred a pair of grey-flannel bags and a pullover. He grinned cheerfully and waved to Joan. And suddenly she was very glad to see him. Glad because he was kind and wholesome and friendly. There were no inhibitions and repressions with him, no inner conflicts, neither difficulties nor bitterness. He was just an ordinary man, in love with her. Anxious to marry her.

In a mood bordering on the hysterical, Joan greeted Ham tonight as a kind of saviour. He, and he alone, could save her from the perpetual torment which she had been forced to bear all these months living in this place with Simon and Sally. He offered the way out. She seized it, recklessly. She did not bother to think or probe any longer. Did not stop to ask herself whether she was not laying up an even greater torment for herself and for Simon. And for an instant she did not even ask herself whether she was being fair to him. When Ham reached her side and asked her to dance she answered:

'Yes, let's dance every one—every single one together. Let's go crazy this evening. That's just how I'm feeling, Ham.'

He looked at her in astonishment. He had never seen Joan in such a mood. The quiet

237

little Miss Parwood was unlike herself—quite transformed, and he had to admit that he'd never seen her look more beautiful. Those large glittering eyes and flaming cheeks took his breath away.

He caught her hand and squeezed it.

'*Hey!* What's come over you?

'Don't ask me,' she said with an hysterical little laugh. 'Just be awfully nice to me, Ham, please.'

William Hamley was a quiet young man, but he felt his heart suddenly knock as he put an arm through hers and led her out of the lounge into the ballroom. Her emotionalism was new and enchanting. He was not one to ask whys or wherefores. He took what the gods offered—when it was offered and gratefully.

The ballroom was deserted and dim. Dancing had not yet commenced. People were going into dinner, and William Hamley seized his chance, for he was an opportunist.

'You don't have to ask me to be nice to you, Joan,' he said, 'you know I'm in love with you and always have been. I don't know what's come over you, but if you want me to propose for the hundredth time . . .'

'I think I do,' said Joan, and blotted out the memory of a thin brown face and two dark, bitter eyes, looking at her with hopeless desire. Simon must not be remembered. What she felt for him, and he for her, must be put into the limbo of forgotten things. If she did not tie herself up quickly, as he was tied, she knew they would both break . . . be ranked with the deserters and the quitters . . . run away together, shamelessly, leaving a woman who was blind.

Joan made a movement towards Ham and the next moment his arms were about her. She pressed her closed eyes against his shoulder. She said in a muffled voice:

'No, Ham, I can't. You're too nice . . .'

'Too nice for what, you silly little thing?'

'Too nice to make use of, my dear. I'm not in love with you—you know that. But I'm fond of you and grateful for your kindness to me, and if . . .'

'If what?'

William Hamley's very blue eyes were shining. It was the first time he had felt Joan's heart beat against his own and he could hardly believe that the miracle had happened, and that she was going to say 'Yes' to him after all.

She said:

'If you really want me to marry you—I will.'

'Gosh!' said Ham in a hushed voice, and then became speechless. She felt his hold of her tighten, felt his lips against her hair, and for an instant she was stricken with remorse and with fear. Remorse because she did not care for this nice man, as he did for her. Fear because she was Simon's . . . so completely Simon's . . . and she felt that she was doing something

239

terrible, unforgivable, allowing another man to touch her; contemplating marriage apart from Simon.

But she had burnt her boats. She could not back out of it now, nor did she really want to. For all these weeks she had been telling herself that it would be the best thing in the world for them all.

She lifted a face to Ham which was no longer glowing. Hysteria had died down in her.

'Ham, my dear, I will try to be what you want, but . . .'

'Don't,' he broke in. 'Don't bother about me. I understand. I know you're needing me. And I want you for my wife, Joan, no matter what your conditions are.'

'You're sweet,' she said brokenly.

He leaned down and kissed her on the lips. It was a gentle, almost brotherly kiss. He was being extraordinarily understanding, she thought. He must have realised how little she wanted passionate caresses tonight.

'We'll celebrate our engagement with a bottle of champagne,' he said, a deep note of excitement in his voice. 'Come along, Joan. You may be Miss Parwood running this hotel, but I'm William Hamley, proprietor of the best garage in the country, and tonight you're dining with me, as my guest, and I'm going to tell the world how lucky I am.'

Joan did not answer him. She allowed him to take her hand and walk with her back into the crowded lounge. She felt like one in a dream. She could not really believe that she had promised to marry this man. Neither could she begin to realise what Simon would feel or say.

She did not really want the world to know what Ham felt. She did not really wish to have this queer, sudden engagement broadcast. But she had no right to stop it. She came out of a kind of daze to find herself facing Simon who had just come downstairs. And then her throat constricted and she had an agonised wish that the ground would open and swallow her up. She heard the two men greet each other. Then Ham said eagerly:

'Will you be the first to congratulate us, Mr. Baxley? Joan and I are going to be married.'

Joan forced herself to look at Simon. He looked back. He was white to the lips. But with admirable self-restraint he smiled and bowed.

'That's grand,' he said. 'I do indeed congratulate you both. Does Sally know?'

'Not yet,' said Ham, and glanced at Joan suddenly doubtful as to whether he had done the right thing in making Simon Roxley the first recipient of their news.

Joan did not look back. Her gaze was still fixed on Simon. Her eyes were silently entreating him to understand and forgive. He gave no sign back. His face was quite cold and mask-like.

241

'Let's find Sally,' he said, 'and all have a drink on it.'

But that was more than Joan could tolerate. She said:

'If you'll excuse me, I was just on my way to the office . . . I am wanted for something.'

'See you both later,' said Simon, and passed on humming a dance tune as though he hadn't a care in the world.

William Hamley was literally dragged to the office by Joan. He could feel her hand hot and shaking in his, and once in that room alone with her, he said:

'Look here. Something's wrong. What's happened between you and Roxley? Something has. That's why you've suddenly promised to marry me, isn't it?'

She sat down at her desk, looking pinched and exhausted as if every bit of vitality had been drained from her body.

'Nothing new has happened. The situation is just as it was.'

Ham seated himself on the desk and lit a cigarette. 'You're still in love with that man,' he said remorselessly.

'Ham, for God's sake.'

'Oh, all right,' he interrupted. 'I won't add to your worries by being bitter. I don't feel bitter. If you're going to marry me, I shall be the happiest man in the world. But I don't want to marry you unless you're perfectly certain you want to go through with it.'

She gave him a beseeching look.

'I'll try to be all you want—Ham—and if you'll give me time.'

'I haven't asked for much, so far, have I?'

'You've been marvellous.'

He leaned across the desk and patted her shoulder in an almost brotherly way.

'Poor little Joan! I think I understand very well. You're wanting a loop-hole of escape. Well, my dear, you can use me to your heart's content. I shall be quite happy about it. But only on condition you tell me if at any time you feel you can't go through with it, and would rather turn back.'

She shook her head dumbly. For an instant she was too overcome to speak. Then she said:

'I don't know why anybody should be as easy as you are.'

'You mean, there isn't anybody who has been as brave as you've been.'

'Oh, Ham.'

And then, in tears, she put a hand up blindly to him. His arm went round her shoulders. He stroked her hair in silence and let her cry for a moment. Then he said:

'I shan't try to step into Roxley's shoes. I'm not such a fool. I'll just try to make you happy, somehow. But will you *swear* though that if you *do* reach breaking-point, you'll tell me?'

She nodded, still speechless.

And as she sat there, feeling his hand upon her hair, listening to his friendly voice, she wondered at the cruelty of life. It was sheer cruelty that she should not be able to love him in the way he deserved . . . and that he must be doomed to love her when her heart belonged to Simon. Oh, that cold, expressionless mask on Simon's face. What in God's name was he really thinking?

She prayed that she would not come face to face with him again that night.

CHAPTER SEVENTEEN

The news of Miss Parwood's engagement to William Hamley spread like wild-fire through the hotel. Joan's friends, his friends, and members of the staff hastened to congratulate them. They were both very popular. And perhaps Joan's tortured spirit would have been more at rest if she had known that the announcement of her engagement did, in some measure, achieve the desired effect upon Simon.

To Simon, the news that William Hamley had broken came as such a blow that it stunned him. For a few seconds only he had been conscious only of overwhelming resentment and anger against Joan. It seemed such flagrant disloyalty in view of their feelings toward each other. And a sensation of jealousy such as he had not thought possible had torn through his very being. Then a queer sort of blackout descended upon him. It was as though nothing seemed to matter very much, nor ever could again. He had lost Joan. Joan was going to marry Hamley. There could be no further question of him running away with her. She was no longer his to look upon with longing and worship. And she no longer wanted his love. She had obviously fallen for this fellow. Well, why not? He was a very nice chap, and she couldn't remain single all her life because of *him.* So that was that, and he had better have a few drinks and get used to it all.

So Simon sat at the bar, and with that stunned feeling remaining, drank a few stiff whiskies, watched a number of pretty girls come in and out, and had a few bets with himself as to which one would leave the man she was with if he, Simon, went up and asked her to dance.

He was just a little drunk—just enough to bemuse his mind, and making him gay and talkative and quite indifferent to his personal griefs—when he joined his wife and the party which she had got together, for dinner.

The party consisted of Sally's usual type of friends. Frivolous and a bit noisy. Simon did not mind. Tonight, he was glad of the noise and frivolity. He had no wish to think. He had no wish to come out of that alcoholic daze, and feel a knife pierce his heart at the thought that

245

he had lost Joan for ever.

Koko had brought his sister down to Great Friars. She sat next to Simon. She was a sophisticated debutante who had had two seasons in town and considered herself a woman of the world. She drank quite a lot but refused to eat much. She was 'slimming' she told Simon confidentially. And very soon they were having quite an intimate talk in which she did most of the confiding, and Simon was most attentive and sympathetic. By the end of dinner, they were in the thick of a desperate flirtation. Bunny Dettering thought Simon Roxley 'fearfully attractive'; she liked his cynical smile and rather sinister way of looking and talking to her. And tonight he was amused by absurdities which ordinarily he would have found boring. Bunny was very pretty. She wore a rose-pink, fluffy dress and a little spangled butterfly was pinned in her dark curls. For a few moments, with his mind rocking, Simon Roxley thought those curls belonged to Joan. He touched the butterfly ornament with a finger and whispered:

'You lovely thing!'

Bunny giggled delightedly and turned to her brother.

'Oh, Koko, Mr. Roxley's being simply *marvellous!*'

Koko stuck his monocle in his eye and looked with some gloom upon Simon. He could see that Sally's husband was not entirely sober. Sally said:

'It's unusual for my husband to be anything but a gloom at a party. You must have fascinated him, Bunny.'

Bunny touched Simon's arm.

'Do I fascinate you?' she asked, looking at him through well-blackened lashes.

'Beyond belief,' said Simon.

Then he saw across the restaurant, a dark-haired girl in a grey dress, sitting alone with a man.

That was Joan. Joan, drinking champagne with Hamley, to celebrate their engagement.

The knife turned and twisted in Simon's heart and soul. Bunny Dettering looked at him anxiously.

How strange he was. Such a queer look had, come across his face.

'Is anything wrong?' she asked.

He sank back into his daze. He was grateful for the drink which he could consume and for the shallow sympathy of the silly little debutante.

'Come and dance, *petite papillon*,' he said unsteadily, 'that's what butterflies were meant for—for dancing. I want to dance, don't you?'

'*Terribly,*' she said, and meant it.

They walked out of the restaurant together towards the ball-room. They had to pass Joan's table. Bunny Dettering, who had met Miss Parwood on a previous visit to Great Friars, nodded and smiled at her gaily. But Simon

247

gave no recognition. Without looking at Joan, he moved past that table and out of her sight.

The Hunt Ball had ended and most of the dancers had left the hotel or retired to bed, before Joan and Simon spoke to each other alone.

For Joan, it had been an exceedingly difficult evening. But she had got through it somehow, and Ham had gone home confident that he could make a success of things with her.

Once she was by herself, Joan found her mind turning to the old tormenting thought of Simon. She had caught sight of him several times during the evening—once or twice with Sally, but most of the time with that pretty child, Bunny Dettering. It had been obvious that they found each other amusing. Now, Sally had retired to her room and Koko and Bunny to theirs. What had happened to Simon, Joan did not know. She was, as usual, the last one to bed. After a show like this, she made it her duty to go round the hotel and see that lights were turned off, and that the night-staff were doing their jobs.

She fancied she saw a light in the bar. That ought to be out. She looked in, then stopped dead on the threshold.

Simon sat on a stool at the bar. He was not thinking. Neither was he smoking. He was just sitting there with his hands in his pockets, his head sunk. That head shot up as Joan appeared. She was shocked by the sight of his face. It was ghastly. She knew that he had drunk more than was good for him tonight. But he was stone-cold sober now. And there was a weariness and disgust in his eyes that hurt her to the soul.

'Oh, Simon!' she said.

He slid off the stool and stood before her. 'Well?' he said.

There was such bitterness in that word that it struck like a blow. She said:

'Did you enjoy yourself this evening?'

He laughed.

'Did you?'

She did not answer. But the blood stung her cheeks and that made him suddenly come to life. He said furiously:

'Why are you marrying that fellow?'

'Because I think it's best, Simon.'

'Best for who? You, me, or him?'

'All of us.'

'Then you're not as intelligent as I thought you were. You don't love him. You love me. How is your marriage going to benefit any of us?'

She shook her head.

'I don't know. But I've got to do it. I've got to get away.'

'You needn't marry William Hamley in order to leave Great Friars.'

'I don't mean that. I mean I've got to get away from myself. Being here doesn't matter any more. And it would be all the same if I were in China.'

'You think because you're engaged to him that it will ease matters?'

'It's got to,' she said desperately.

'Does he know how you feel?'

'Yes, and understands.'

'Well, he may be a fool, but I don't blame him for taking what the gods offer. They didn't offer it to me.'

'Simon,' said Joan in a heartrending voice, 'I beg and implore you not to make things any harder for me or for yourself.'

He shrugged his shoulders.

'My dear Joan, I'm not going to ask you to remain single for my sake. I'm sure it will be all for the best if you marry Hamley . . . But don't delude yourself that it will make *my* lot any easier. I shall remain with Sally, and I shall be as good as dead.'

She shook her head, speechlessly. There seemed nothing to say. He added:

'Except when I'm tight enough to make myself attractive to pretty girls like Bunny Dettering, who has as much soul as the butterfly in her hair.'

Still Joan made no reply. She felt very tired. If her engagement, her marriage to Ham would not make Simon's lot any easier, how could it ease her own particular load?

'What have I done?' she asked herself. 'What have I done?'

Simon took a step toward her.

'When first I heard your news, I thought that you had fallen for Hamley. But that isn't true, is it?'

'No,' she whispered.

'Then what you're going to do is a mistake, Joan.'

She covered her face with her hands.

'I thought it would be for the best.'

Sudden tenderness seized him. In this early morning hour, alone with her, and face to face with facts, Simon Roxley felt neither resentment nor desire. But he was more than ever before conscious of immense love for Joan. He took her in his arms and pressed his lips against her cheek. He felt it cold and wet with tears.

'My poor sweet,' he said, 'I have behaved like a swine. I've driven you to this. I haven't behaved at all well. All you want is peace. I think I understand. And I hope to God you'll find it. I think I could almost be happy if I thought you were to be happy at last. But I'm so afraid you won't be—with him.'

She clung to Simon, weeping.

'Oh, darling, darling, I don't know what to do.'

'Don't worry, darling. Give it a trial. He may be the way out that you're wanting. Give it a trial.'

'But I love you!' she said. 'Simon, I couldn't love anybody else. I must be mad to do what I did tonight.'

'Give it a trial,' he repeated, 'and I'll see what I can do on my side to make things easy for you both. I haven't been very unselfish so far. I'm afraid I've been concentrating on my own misery.'

She gave a shuddering sigh and looked up with wild, wet eyes. He kissed her on the mouth.

'I shall love you forever,' he said, 'believe that.'

'Simon, *Simon* . . .'

'It's all too difficult for us, my sweet. And this sort of love doesn't seem to bring happiness. I wonder sometimes if it pays to be serious-minded. Koko and Bunny—their sort are happy. And in her way, poor blind Sally is happy, too.'

'But I'd rather be me,' whispered Joan, 'loving you and loved by you, even without hope.'

'You couldn't say anything nicer than that.'

For an instant they stood there, in a close embrace. And during those moments, despair and pain were wiped out. They were very much one and at peace. But it was a fleeting respite. They had to say 'good night', Joan told herself, and this time 'good-bye'. For tomorrow she must embark upon her new existence as the future wife of William Hamley, and her loyalty must be to him, and never again must she know the perfection of Simon's kiss, Simon's embrace.

Perhaps you've done the right thing, Joan,' were his last words to her. 'We'll both see how things work out, and for God's sake don't let my love for you, or, yours for me, hurt you any more.'

And it was on that note that they parted. A new heroic note for Simon. Yet both of them knew, from the moment they separated, that there could be neither peace nor happiness for them, apart from one another.

CHAPTER EIGHTEEN

It was about a fortnight later that a man with a foreign accent telephoned from London to the Great Friars hotel to book a suite for himself and his family. A man who at first seemed of no importance to Joan Parwood, except as another guest who would pay well. He was an Austrian—apparently Jewish. He had escaped from Vienna on the night before Hitler marched into Austria. His wife was English, and they appeared to have plenty of money. They took the most expensive rooms in the hotel. It was explained to Joan, who spoke to them, that their young son was recovering from an appendix operation and they wished him to stay in the country, quietly for Christmas.

253

It was not until the exiled family had arrived and been installed at the hotel that the news leaked out that Herr Rosenstein was an ophthalmic surgeon, and one-time famous specialist in Vienna. The first person to hear the news was Sally. Sally at once sent for Joan.

'I'd like to talk to this man, Joan,' she said. 'I've always had a belief in the Austrians or Germans, and I think that the Jews are the cleverest people in the world. Rosenstein might not agree with the others, that I shall never recover my sight.'

Joan looked with pity at the other girl. Such moments as these could not fail to inspire her with compassion, although lately Sally had been so selfish and irritable that she had made life wretched for everyone who came in contact with her. And Joan could see no use in fostering any wild hope in Sally about her eyes. She had seen half the big men in Europe, and they had all shaken their heads.

'Why don't you answer?' demanded Sally.

'My dear, talk to him by all means, but . . .'

'But you think it's hopeless?'

'What's hopeless?' said a third voice, and Simon walked into the private sitting-room. Simon had just come down from town. He looked cold and dispirited. It was wretched weather—ice and fog, and his train was half an hour late. He went straight across to the fire and spread his hands out to the blaze, barely looking at either of the two girls.

Joan gave him only a fleeting glance. Since her engagement to Ham, two weeks ago, she had done her level best to do what she considered the right thing, and had seen as little of Simon as possible. As far as she knew, he had endeavoured to do likewise.

'It's about my eyes,' said Sally, in the impatient voice which she generally used to her husband, 'I want to talk to that Austrian who was turned out of Vienna. I hear he was considered a genius over there, and he's going to practise in this country.'

Simon lit a cigarette.

'What Austrian? Didn't know there was one in the hotel.'

'You never know anything,' said Sally pettishly; 'tell him, Joan.'

Joan said:

'Mr. Rosenstein is that little man with gold-rimmed glasses and square, baldish head. You may have seen him in the restaurant.'

Simon hadn't seen him. He was not in the mood these days to notice anything or anybody. He had been suffering a little hell of his own since William Hamley put that diamond engagement-ring on Joan's finger. But he was at once interested in what Joan had to say about Rosenstein.

'By all means Sally ought to see him. She oughtn't to leave any stone unturned to get back her sight. But, my dear . . .' he addressed his wife '. . . don't build up too much hope. It'll

255

only upset you if he agrees with the rest'

Sally stamped her foot,

'Oh, don't be so gloomy. Why shouldn't I hope? If I thought I had to go on with this wretched life I lead here, I'd commit suicide.'

'Sorry you feel like that,' said Simon. 'I do my best . . .'

'Oh, I'm sure you do,' broke in Sally, 'but you don't amuse me.'

'Neither does it amuse me to come home every night to be nagged at,' flashed Simon.

Joan thought:

'Oh, God, another scene! It's so horrible . . . I have to stand by and watch it all, and suffer too . . .'

'Joan!' came from Sally in a peremptory voice, 'tell Mr. Rosenstein about my accident, and say I want to see him.'

'All right, darling, I will.'

Joan met Simon's gaze for the flash of an instant. Only a flash . . . his unhappy eyes conveying their message of hopeless love. Then Joan hurried out. Clenching her hand, the sharp diamond of her ring bit into the flesh. It jerked her out of her own pain into remembrance of Ham whom she was going to marry, and who was so happy because of it. And it seemed to her as it had seemed for the last fourteen days and nights, that she had done the maddest thing in pitching herself into that engagement.

Ham had been marvellous. Once or twice

she had tried to give herself up to the sheer physical side of things . . . had tried to find comfort in his arms and his lips. But she had failed because the ghost of Simon was always there between them. And she knew that she could love nobody save him. And Ham knew that too. How long he would be content with such a one-sided bargain, she did not know.

She tried to concentrate on the thought of Rosenstein and Sally's eyes. Supposing by some miracle this little Austrian Jew who had found his way to Great Friars was the one man in the world who could cure her? Supposing Sally *did* recover her sight. What then? Ten chances to one she would at once separate from Simon. Or he would leave her. They had drifted so hopelessly apart already. They had nothing in common. When first they had met, pleasure-seeking, inconsequent, things had been different. But Simon later had realised his mistake, only to find himself forced into marrying her because of her accident. Should it ever happen that she could see again and was no longer in need of his protection and fidelity, *would he stay with her!* Or, if Sally, could find a man like Keith Dettering to go to, would she stay with Simon?

Exciting, dangerous thoughts. Thoughts to make Joan's heart shake, and her cheeks change from red to white. Only to remind herself that even if Simon were free, it would be too late. This time it was *she* who was tied.

She told herself to stop thinking altogether. It was sheer madness.

She walked through the lounge of the hotel, It was cocktail-time. Frau Rosenstein and her little son had probably gone to their rooms to dress for dinner. But the great little man was there, seated in a chair, studying an illustrated magazine, a large meerschaum in the corner of his mouth.

As Joan approached him, she was suddenly conscious of futility. Why should this little bald-headed man have the power to restore Sally's sight, when some of the most brilliant surgeons in the world had failed?

But Sally wished to see him. So Joan did as she was asked.

'Herr Rosenstein . . .' she said.

He looked up, removed his pipe and rose to his feet, clicking them together and bowing with the unimpeachable manners of his race.

'Fraulein.'

'Could I speak to you for a moment?' she asked.

'But, of course,' he said in his excellent English, smiling, and indicated the chair beside him,

Like everybody else who came to Great Friars, he was an admirer of the attractive and very efficient young woman who managed the place.

Within a very few minutes, Joan had secured the desired result. The little man, once a famous and sought-after opinion in the country which would not now accept him because of his religion, expressed a keen interest in the case of Mrs. Simon Roxley. He questioned Joan closely about the accident and all that had since transpired. He seemed acquainted personally with quite a number of the men whom Sally had already consulted. Sir Metford Kilwick he knew and admired. He had read the Englishman's book on ophthalmic surgery and incidentally, he told Joan that he was much afraid that he, Rosenstein, could not hope to succeed where others had failed.

Joan argued that it was not so much a question of success and failure as of opinion. None of these men had attempted to operate. They had just said it would be no use. But why shouldn't somebody try? Things couldn't be worse than they were now. There poor Sally was—young and beautiful—and blind.

Rosenstein agreed that it was a colossal tragedy. He was only too willing to see Mrs. Roxley. He was not practising in this country yet, but he would be delighted to give his private opinion and convey any conclusion that he reached to Sir Metford Kwick.

'You know, of course,' said Rosenstein, 'with detached retina, it is a question of finding a hole, without which no operation would avail?'

'I know that,' said Joan. 'It was all explained

to us after the accident.'

Rosenstein knocked the bowl of his pipe against an ash-tray beside him.

'*Ach,* well! We will see what we will see. It is fortunate that I have with me my tools . . . my thermoscope. And after dinner, if Mrs. Roxley wishes it so, I will be at her disposal.'

Joan rang through to Sally's suite to convey this information to her. Sally became suddenly, madly excited. It was months since she had seen an oculist. She was thrown into the wildest state of renewed hope by the mere fact that a celebrated oculist was staying in the hotel and had consented to examine her.

Her condition made Simon very gentle with her. Sally had been putting him through a bad time, but she was, after all, such a child. Almost as young and frivolous and silly in her way as that sister of Koko's. He did not want her to hope too much. He would loathe to see her flung back into the old nightmare of despair over the terrible affliction which she had never learned to accept philosophically.

Sally's excitement gradually communicated itself to Simon. In anticipation of the Austrian's opinion, he could hardly eat his own dinner, and Joan felt the same emotion. She had been going out with Ham to visit some friends of his in Maidenhead. She put him off. She must be upstairs with Sally when Rosenstein made his examination.

'Good Lord,' said Ham over the telephone

when she spoke to him, 'you don't mean that there's a chance . . .'

'We don't know. It is probably quite crazy of us to let him see Sally and upset her for nothing.' Joan cut in, 'but there it is. He had a huge reputation in Vienna, and if Sally wants to see him, she must.'

'Well, jolly good luck to it,' said Ham, then added: 'I haven't seen much of *you* these last few days, darling.'

'I've been busy,' she said.

'Well, don't be too busy to spare me a moment, soon.'

'Come round later,' said Joan, and hung up.

But she regretted the invitation as soon as she had made it. She had less wish than usual to see Ham tonight, and make the effort to please him. Heavens, what an evening it would be! Rosenstein would probably endorse the opinion of the other men on Sally, then there would be the devil to pay with her all night.

Sally was quite hysterical by the time the little Austrian doctor made his call. As soon as he entered the room and she heard his voice, she began to ply him with questions. Did he think there was any hope? Had he had another case like hers? Couldn't he operate? Why had the others not had a go at it? Why should she be doomed to blindness for the rest of her life? Etc., etc.

Simon held one of her hands and Joan the other. She snatched them both away and

261

clutched frantically at Rosenstein's arm. Anxiously Joan and Simon looked at each other and at the Austrian. He was smiling and unconcerned. And in a few moments he had Sally completely under control. He had a soothing voice and manner and he had obviously dealt with similar temperaments in his long and varied career. His eyes beamed at Sally behind their powerful glasses.

'So!' he said softly. 'Such very beautiful eyes, my child. It would be indeed a pity that the light should be extinguished in them for ever. Come, sit down and let me look at them more closely.'

Sally was quiet. She allowed Rosenstein to do as he wished. She sat down and the little man gave directions about the electric lamps.

Joan and Simon found themselves sitting together on the sofa. They did not look at each other. With bated breath, they just sat and watched and waited. In some queer way, Rosenstein was putting them all under a spell.

During that spell Joan's own consciousness seemed to float out of the room into another world. It was as though she was in total darkness, but she could feel Simon's presence beside her. That was strangely comforting. She was only dimly conscious of the shapes in front of her. The shape of Rosenstein lifting instruments out of his bag, and Sally's golden head flung backwards, her white faced carved into a mask of terrible hope.

Then a hand enfolded Joan's. Simon's hand. She could feel his fingers dry and shaking. Her own fingers twined about his. They sat there in that queer silence, holding on to each other, hearing only the tinkle of instruments in Rosenstein's case.

Then Joan was jerked back to complete realisation of all that was going on. For Rosenstein spoke:

'May I have all the lights on again, please?' Simon released Joan's hand, got up and moved to the switch.

Joan blinked and looked from Rosenstein to Sally. She had never known her heart to beat so fast. It was Sally who asked the question which was uppermost in the minds of the other two.

'Well? Is there any hope? *Is* there?'

Rosenstein stood silent a moment, as though pondering. Then he snapped the catch of his bag together and said:

'It is my opinion that there is hope.'

Another silence. It was broken by a cry from Sally.

'*Simon! Joan!* Did you hear that?'

Joan sprang up and went to her friend and put an arm about her.

'My dear . . .' and then stopped, for no other words would come.

Simon, very white, looked at Rosenstein. 'You really think that, sir?'

The Austrian nodded.

'With an operation, I think that the sight of one eye at least could be restored. There is a hole in the retina of the right eye. Of the left, I am not so hopeful.

Another cry from Sally, half-laughing, half-crying.

'I don't care a damn about the left, if the right can be restored. I only ask for the sight of one. But to see *at all.* Oh, *God,* wouldn't that be wonderful?'

Simon crossed to her side and took one of her hands.

'It would be very wonderful, darling,' he said, huskily.

'I would like,' said Rosenstein, 'to get in touch with Sir Metford Kilwick tomorrow, and convey my opinion and ask him to examine Mrs. Roxley again—with me.'

Sally tore her fingers from Simon's.

'I don't care *what* he says. If you think there's hope, you've got to operate. You've *got to.* Oh, you will, won't you?'

'*Ja, ja,*' said Rosenstein, 'if it is the wish of your husband and yourself, and I have every hope that Sir Metford will support me, and change his opinion about that right eye.'

It was a night that none of them would forget. Virtually the turning point in the lives of them all. It was a night on which Sally and her husband might have been brought together—would have been—if Sally had behaved differently. For Simon was deeply touched by her pathetic joy, and anxious to share in it. But it was not with him that Sally shared that ecstasy of hope. It was with the man who was responsible for her blindness. In some curious way she had lost her need for Simon. It was Koko with his inanities, his futile expressions, his disregard of the serious side of life, whom she needed, and for whom she sent. She telephoned to him wildly, begging him to come straight down to the hotel. She telephoned to her father. Half the night she spent in making calls to her personal friends, broadcasting the opinion of the German oculist.

Koko came, anxious to express his enthusiasm in his own way with as many drinks as he could swallow, and armfuls of flowers for Sally.

Sally was like a lunatic and nothing that Simon or Joan could say could quieten her down. They both shared the same terror that Rosenstein's opinion might be wrong, and then Sally's last state would be worse than her first. Any effort that they made to reason with her resulted in rage or jibes.

'A couple of wet blankets,' she flung at them. She did not want either of them in her room. So Simon walked out of the room and out of the hotel, knowing that Sally blind, or with sight regained, could never mean anything to him again. And Joan spent the evening with Ham, filled with the intolerable longing to follow Simon and comfort him, yet knowing that she must not.

Following that night, came others equally heart-shaking and momentous for them all.

Sally's father arrived and drove her and Rosenstein up to London, where a consultation was held in Sir Metford Kilwick's house.

The result of that consultation was telephoned to Simon at his office and to Joan at the hotel. And it was then that they all really began to hope. For the English oculist agreed with the Austrian. Months ago when he had first examined Sally, he had not found that necessary hole in the retina of either eye, but now he could see it. He was in accordance with Rosenstein that an operation might restore the sight of that right eye, although the left would remain as it was.

Twenty-four hours later, Sally was in a nursing home, and the great little Austrian Jew, himself, operated, assisted by Metford Kilwick.

There had been no question of anything else. Metford Kilwick bowed to a greater opinion than his own. He was a much younger man than Rosenstein. And years before his own book had been written, he had studied Rosenstein's works on Ophthalmic Surgery, and helped to educate himself with them.

The result of that operation was entirely successful. For Sally Roxley, hope became fact. The day dawned when the bandages were removed and she who had lived in total darkness since that crash at Cockmarsh, saw the light again. Saw it only with one eye which had to learn to focus like two, but *she could see.* At first, faint shapes and forms, then clearly the people and things which had been obscured from her for what seemed an eternity. Her father's face . . . his was the first she saw . . . Then Simon's, then Joan's and Keith Dettering's. And it was Koko's which meant the most. Once alone with him, it was into Koko's willing arms that she fell, crazy with delight. And he who said all the gay, silly things that she wanted to hear.

'Oh, *boy,* won't we make whoopee now!' he exclaimed, almost as much beside himself as Sally. 'You don't know what this means to me, when I remember what happened to you was my fault. Boy, *oh, boy!* isn't this grand? Are you sure you can see again?'

'Positive!'

'Then there are a whole lot of things you're going to focus on straight away. The Ritz-bar, Luigi's Grill and a show or a cinema or a cabaret or . . . '

The Hon. Koko paused, grimacing.

'What's the matter?' said Sally.

'I was forgetting. You've got a husband.'

Then Sally became thoroughly sincere.

'I may have one, but he's the wrong husband for me, Koko. And he's no more pleased with me than I am with him. It's my belief that he'd be only too glad if somebody removed me straight out of the way.'

Koko scratched his cheek.

'H'm, I shouldn't be surprised. It was never really a "go", was it?'

'Never. Simon has a conscience, and I think he married me because of it.'

'Then what do you say if we step into my motorcar and stage a nice run-away,' said Koko.

Sally looked at him with shining eyes. She was still so enraptured with her returned sight that Koko appeared to her positively handsome, added to which she told herself he was her *kind,* and he *had* heaps of money and a title; if she left Simon, her father would see that he and the Roxley's didn't suffer financially. For after all, a bargain was a bargain, and the Roxleys were broke.

She ruffled Koko's hair with unsteady fingers, and said:

'I'm all for a quick fade-out with you, Koko. The sooner the better.'

So it was that night—the first night on which Sally could really see again—that she left her London flat in Koko's car, never to return to it.

CHAPTER NINETEEN

The day on which Sally Roxley ran away with the Hon. Keith Dettering, was full of moment for the Simon Roxleys on both sides of the family. For almost before Simon had recovered from the not unpleasant shock of hearing that his wife, after recovering her sight, had decided to leave him, his father suddenly died.

Old Sir George had been out shooting. He was a fine sportsman of the old type and never gave in until the end. His was the finale which he would have chosen, gun in hand and a spaniel at his heels. Just a sudden heart-attack blotting out the sight of the pheasants, and dimming for ever for him the voice of his keeper calling: *'Mark o-v-e-r!'*

They took him home and telephoned to the new master of Roxley Hall. So Simon, within a few hours of emerging from the chaos of Sally's departure, found himself plunged into the much more tragic loss of a beloved parent. When he was able to think dearly, he found it ironic that he should have become Sir Simon on the very day that Sally abandoned him. She had always coveted the title. But of course there was now a likelihood of her having an even bigger one. Well, he wouldn't begrudge it to her, neither would he pretend to be sorry that she had gone. Their brief marriage had not been a success. But he felt bitter resentment at the thought of these months which had been wasted; the frightful waste of loyalty and sacrifice for her sake. It had all been to no good. He had lost Joan at the beginning, and now when it was all over he must lose her again because she was going to marry somebody else.

But it was some long time before he could think of his personal emotions. He was much too busy at Roxley Hall. Following his father's funeral, there was the disagreeable business of serving divorce papers upon Sally and Koko. Then of settling up the Roxley estate—without Sally's money.

A conference with his young brother Vivian resulted in both of them agreeing that they could not accept any more money from the Vaughans. Old Vaughan, as Sally had anticipated, thoroughly angry at his daughter's behaviour, expressed himself willing, to continue paying some of his fortune into the Roxley estate. But Simon would have none of it. He had never been happy about using Sally's money. In the very beginning, while they had cared for each other, things had seemed different, but now that she was going to belong to somebody else, he could not tolerate the thought of accepting her father's charity.

There were, of course, certain benefits

from his title and estate, but he would have to sell Roxley Hall and Vivian must resign from the army. It was hard on the boy, but Vivian was ready and willing to do it. There was the possibility of a job for him with the insurance firm for whom Simon was now working.

Thus it happened that with so much afoot, Simon and Joan did not meet until long, after Christmas had come and another year commenced.

It was a shattering Christmas for Joan. There was the usual effort of double work at the hotel during the festivities of the season. Added to that, she had to unravel the tangle which Sally left behind her. All her things were sorted and packed and sent to her father's house. All correspondence had to be directed to her, care of Dettering. The pair had gone to Cannes where they had been lent a villa, and they expected to remain there until the decree was made absolute.

It was Sally, herself, who broke the news of her departure to Joan. The two girls had a long talk on the telephone. Sally said:

'I daresay you think I'm very wicked and all the rest of it, and it does look as though I'm ungrateful to Simon for being so good to me while I was blind. But I don't really feel guilty, because I can't, somehow, believe that he'll really mind. What do you think?'

Joan could not begin to say what she thought. She was much too dazed. And it seemed such a cruelty of fate that Simon should be set free now when she had given her word to another. And only given it because she had loved Simon too much. For that, which seemed a paradox, was the simple truth. It was her intense love for Simon that had driven her to Ham.

Sally begged Joan to stay on at the hotel and run it with her usual efficiency.

Joan found herself imploring Sally to make sure that she was doing the right thing; to think well over her actions before it was too late to retract.

'This may be just a moment of hysteria,' she said. 'You have only just got back your sight. Everything must seem intoxicating. For God's sake do nothing rash until you've calmed down.'

But Sally was not to be moved from her resolution to run away with Koko. They had so much in common, and so she told Joan, it was Koko whom she would have chosen at the beginning, had he, instead of Simon, proposed to her then.

So Joan said good-bye to Sally. Then within a bewilderingly short space of time, came the news of Sir George's death, and Simon's new responsibilities.

With Christmas, there arrived a gift and a letter from him.

The gift was a lovely old sapphire brooch in an antique setting. It had belonged to Simon's mother. He wrote:

'I am selling up everything and came across this, which I remember my mother wearing. I would like you to have it as a Christmas gift, and with my thanks for your wonderful, untiring services to Sally. I hope and believe that Hamley will not mind you taking this from me. One day I suppose I shall feel that I can come down to Great Friars and see you again, but for the moment I can't. I hope you will understand.

Ever yours,
SIMON.'

Joan wrote back her thanks for that gift, but she felt that she would never be able to let him know how deeply touched she was by his thought in giving her such a valuable momenta of his mother, whom she knew he had adored. But when she addressed the envelope with the unfamiliar title: *'Sir Simon Roxley,'* her heart ached unbearably. Poor lonely Simon! How unutterably wretched he must be now, she thought. If he felt as she imagined he did, how frightful it was that she could not be with him to help him now.

Bitterly she reproached herself for the rash manner in which she had tied herself up to Ham. But having a particularly stubborn conscience, she never for a moment considered throwing Ham over because Simon was free.

She was tender and patient with her fiancé these days. He could never complain of her attitude. But nothing escaped William Hamley. He was much too truly fond of Joan, as well as passionately attracted by her, to let anything escape him. When she asked his permission to wear Simon's brooch, she asked it with studied carelessness, but he could see her colour change and the fingers that held the brooch for his inspection, tremble a little.

But he did nothing for the moment. He was not a man to move hastily. And perhaps at the back of his mind he had a forlorn hope that, given time, Joan's feeling for Roxley would eventually change.

So, for Joan, the new year dawned bleakly. She went through the cold and damp of January days feeling that she was having to force body and brain to go on, and repress every natural instinct. She wondered how long it would be before she cracked up under the strain.

She was near to breaking point, when, one grey, foggy day—a Sunday—Simon came down to Great Friars for the first time since Sally's elopement and his father's death.

It was the faithful Andy who rushed into the office to announce excitedly that Sir Simon was on his way in to see Miss Parwood.

Joan, who had been like one dead, sprang suddenly to life, at the mere mention of that name. When Simon walked into her office, she was speechless for a moment, and could only look at him. And he, closing the door behind him, looked back and was also without words.

Both of them were struck by the same thought . . . how the other had changed . . .

To Joan, Simon seemed to have grown taller and slighter. There was nothing left of the gay, cynical boy whom she had first met. Here was a mature man with stern lips and eyes, whose cares seemed to sit heavily upon him. Why, she even detected a touch of grey in the raven-black hair on either side of his temples. And he found her more frail than before—so much too thin and white and big-eyed—his poor little Joan! What happiness, in God's name, he asked himself, had she found with Hamley? To what purpose was that engagement? It was futile like everything else. The whole history of their love was one of tragic futility.

Yet now, when they saw each other, after months of separation, they were both fully conscious that their love was unchanged. As vital, as compelling, as intense as ever.

And no repressions, no control kept them out of each other's arms. He came swiftly to her side and like a flash she was in his embrace, responsive and eager for his kisses, which he rained wildly on her eyes and lips and hair.

'My sweet, my *sweet*,' he murmured between those long hungry kisses.

And she buried her face against his shoulder and held him close, whispering:

'Simon, oh, Simon, my *darling.*'

But as swiftly as passion had overwhelmed them, they drew apart. They looked at each other with conscience-stricken gaze. Then Simon seated himself on the edge of the desk—a position so familiar—took out a cigarette case and handed it to her.

'Better smoke, eh?'

With shaking fingers she took a cigarette from the case. After she had lit it, she smoothed back her tumbled hair and ran a powder-puff over her flushed face. A face which all too soon lost its burning glow, and took on the old pallor.

'That was all wrong,' she said under her breath.

'The whole darn thing's wrong, Joan.'

She tried to laugh.

'We're being very unoriginal. We seem to have said things like this before.'

He looked down at the point of his cigarette. 'I must apologise.'

'For heaven's sake, don't.'

'I oughtn't to have come down,' were his next words.

For an instant she did not answer. In one way she was so terribly pleased to see him, and in another she knew that he was right. It would have been better if he had not come. It was like reopening a wound, long before it had really healed.

What he really felt she could only guess from the impulsive passion of his greeting. But she knew well enough that she personally had been dying slowly of that wound, for endless weeks.

With the old moody look, he glanced round the little office. Nothing had changed here. Joan had not really changed, standing there in her overall of faded green tussore silk. There on the desk was her familiar array of papers and ledgers. There was a glass bowl too, full of forced daffodils. A touch of spring, yellow and enchanting, in the gloom of the January afternoon. And out there through the windows, behind the fog, the bulbs were lying under the mud in the lovely garden of the hotel, waiting to burst forth into bloom. Soon it would be February, then Spring would come and there would be sunshine, flowers and all the beauty and promise of new growth, new life. But for him, and for Joan, there would be nothing but sterility. Everything was doomed to die—all their love and their longing.

He felt suddenly furious with himself for losing his control and allowing himself to think this way. Living down at Roxley Hall with his brother and working hard at the office every day, he fancied he had gained some sort of peace and that he would learn to face life alone, without this loved woman. As soon as the summer came and his decree was made absolute, he meant to take a holiday abroad and find some new distraction.

But he realised that it was all no good. Life could and would mean nothing without Joan. How hellish it was, he thought, that when last he had been here, Sally had stood between them. Now, Sally had gone and there was another very solid barrier—William Hamley.

Gloomily he fixed his gaze upon the ring on Joan's finger.

'I don't know why I did come down,' he said abruptly, 'something drove me here, I suppose—some wish to see you. But now I'd better go away and stay away, hadn't I?'

She was dead white now.

'Wouldn't you stay to dinner?' she asked painfully.

'What—a meal *à trois* with your fiancé?'

The sarcasm stung her.

'Don't be beastly, Simon.'

'I'm sorry,' he muttered, 'but honestly, Joan, I'd better clear out.'

She swallowed hard.

'Won't you let me even hear your news?'

He shrugged his shoulders.

'There isn't much. I have had a tremendous lot to do—just as well, perhaps. Vivian's home, you know, and with me in the office, I think he'll do well.'

'You're doing very well, aren't you?'

'Better than I'd hoped. There are a lot of damned snobs in the firm and they like my

278

title.'

'Do you like it?' she asked with a ghost of a smile.

'It means nothing to me, my dear.'

She sighed.

'I daresay not. Is your brother frightfully disappointed about the Army?'

'He was at first, but we're both quite pleased not to be dependent upon any money from Vaughan.'

'Have you heard from . . .?'

'From Sally?' he finished, with a twisted smile. 'Yes. She is an extraordinary person. She writes quite often to say how much she is enjoying life with Koko. She's like an inconsequent child. Quite inhuman at times, and I don't think she has any heart. Her blindness might have given her one, but it didn't. It made her worse than she was. Well, it doesn't matter now. Let her be happy. I'm better off alone.'

Then he added:

'When are you going to be married?'

If ever Joan's heart had been near to breaking, it seemed to break in that moment. She felt that she was being loyal almost beyond endurance. She broke out with unaccustomed passion:

'I ought never to marry Ham at all—I *oughtn't*, feeling as I do:

'Then why do it?'

Simon shot the question so unexpectedly at

279

her that for the moment she had no answer. He went on:

'All this sacrifice—all this doing the right thing—it can be overdone. It's the stuff for heroes and heroines in magazines. You may be a heroine, but, God! I'm no hero, Joan, and never have been. I love you and I know you love me. You promised to marry Hamley because you were afraid of things as they were when Sally was my wife. But I very much doubt whether you have the right to go on hurting Hamley. Why not be more afraid of hurting me?'

She shook her head.

'You don't understand. I loathe hurting you. And I don't like hurting myself. But I gave Ham my word . . .'

'Then ask him to release you.'

'It wouldn't be fair.'

'It isn't fair either way,' said Simon.

Somebody knocked on the office door.

Joan pulled herself together, remembered that she was manageress of this place, and said: 'Come in'—Simon walked to the window, looked out at the thickening fog and wondered how long it would take him to drive back to Roxley Hall and why the devil he had tortured himself and Joan, by coming here at all.

A boy from Hamley's garage walked into the office with a note for Joan.

'There's no answer, Miss,' he grinned at her. Joan, recognising Ham's writing said:

'Where is Mr. Hamley, Peter?'

'He's just gone off, Miss. Down to Eastbourne for the night.'

'All right,' said Joan. 'Thanks, Peter.'

The boy departed. Perplexed, Joan opened the flap of the envelope. Ham's old mother lived at Eastbourne. Was the old lady ill? Why hadn't Ham telephoned her? They were supposed to be having supper together tonight.

She read what he had written. Simon, lighting another cigarette, watched, feasting his gaze on the sight of her slender beauty, wondering when he would see her again once he had said goodbye.

With a queer look in her eyes, she handed him the letter.

'We've just agreed that it isn't fair either way,' she said slowly, 'and Ham seems to know that too. As you said, we are not the stuff that heroes or heroines are made of, but this note has been written by a man whom I think can truly be called heroic.'

Simon put his cigarette in the ash-tray and picked up the letter. Ham had an untidy, school-boy writing. He seemed to have written this letter in a great hurry. It said:

'Joan darling. Have just seen Roxley's car drive past. I know exactly what is going to happen. You two are going to be noble and say goodbye, and then you're going to be more noble and carry on with your

marriage to me. But I'm not accepting the martyrdom, honey. I'm not that sort of chap.

'It was all right when Roxley's wife was in the way. I thought I might be a help to you. I've been thinking a lot about it ever since she bunked off with Dettering. And now I've come to a decision. I'm not going to marry you, my dear. You're going to be free to take the happiness you've always wanted. Tell Roxley I said so, and wish him luck for me. And don't try to alter my decision, because it won't work.

'I am going down to my mother for a day or two. Don't worry about me. I hate losing you, but you're such a grand girl, I'd like to see you again and see you really happy. Good luck, darling, and don't forget to patronise the old garage when you're Lady Roxley.

Just the same.
HAM.'

Simon came to the signature and looked up at Joan. Her eyes were swimming with tears. He, himself, could not but feel touched by that letter. But man-like he was first and foremost thrilled by the exquisite thought that Joan had been given her freedom.

'God!' he said in a hushed voice, 'How marvellous! I can't believe it's true.'

'It's so like him; said Joan, with a choked

voice. 'Oh, Simon, he really is the grandest person alive.'

'I take my hat off to him,' said Simon, 'God knows I do.'

Still Joan's conscience held her back.

'How can I let him go off like this . . .'

Simon came to her side and took both her hands.

'Sweet, you can't do anything else. He's right. He doesn't want you to be a martyr. You were meant to marry me. You're *going* to marry me. Say it, for heavens sake.'

Then she hesitated no longer.

She knew that he was right and that Ham was right. Always she had loved Simon. She must love him until she died. She could belong to no other man. In her heart she had known that all the time.

She moved into Simon's arms and for the first time for long weary months she was at peace. With her cheek pressed to his, she whispered; 'If you want me still . . . you know I'm yours.'

'There's no "if" about it, dearest. I've never stopped wanting you. We need only say goodbye for a little while. I shall be free at the end of the summer, and then, let us make what we can of life together, my sweet.'

She smoothed the black, handsome head with both hands and looked up through her tears into the dark glowing eyes of the man who meant life itself to her.

'I don't mind how long I have to wait, when I know that in the end we shall be together. I'll stay here and work. I like being here in a way. And I think somehow that Ham's capable of becoming a real friend again like he used to be. You could never be jealous of Ham now, could you?'

'How could I? I shall write and thank him for the gift of you. I realise that without his making the move, you would never have broken your word, and I would never have won you. As I think I told you long ago, my sweet, you're quite frightening in your strength.'

'You don't know how weak I feel—in your arms.'

'I do love you so,' he said passionately, 'I love you so much that I don't know how I'm going to live without seeing you till my divorce is through.'

'You can write every day,' she said happily, 'and perhaps sometimes we can speak on the 'phone.'

'I think Miss Parwood will be answering so many toll-calls that she will find her work seriously interrupted.'

They laughed together. Joan wondered how long it was since she had heard Simon laugh at all.

An hour later, they found that the fog was lifting. They could see the shapes of the old trees in the garden, and the alders down by the river.

'It's a good omen,' said Simon, as he walked with Joan through the lounge to his car. 'The fog is lifting from us, forever. When I see you again, my sweet—I hope the sun will be shining, and we shall meet—say at Caxton Hall with Vivian and any friend whom you care to bring.

Her heart seemed to turn over at the thought of that day—her marriage-day with Simon.

'I shall bring Andy,' she said. 'Andy's one of the best friends I've ever had, and I think she has known all along how I've felt about you.'

'I think the one person who doesn't know it is Sally,' said Simon, as he opened the door of his car and began to draw on his gauntlets. 'I really do think, Joan, whatever we've done, we can have full marks for our behaviour while she was here!'

'Oh, I agree. And I think we'll both be glad that we didn't let her down when she was blind. But there's Ham . . .'

'Darling,' he interrupted, 'I don't think you need feel that you've let Ham down, either. He understands and he doesn't want you to let *yourself* down. Now do promise you'll be happy, and stop worrying about anything.'

'I couldn't be anything but happy now, Simon, my darling.'

He raised her hand to his lips and took his place at the wheel of his car.

'Good night,' he said, 'and goodbye until we

meet again—on our wedding-day.'

She stood there outside the hotel, and watched the car drive through the ever-lifting grey whorls of mist. When she turned and walked back into the warmth and light of the lounge, it seemed as though she was moving, breathing, living in a new enchanted world.

Chivers Large Print Direct

If you have enjoyed this Large Print book and would like to build up your own collection of Large Print books and have them delivered direct to your door, please contact **Chivers Large Print Direct**.

Chivers Large Print Direct offers you a full service:

☆ **Created to support your local library**

☆ **Delivery direct to your door**

☆ **Easy-to-read type and attractively bound**

☆ **The very best authors**

☆ **Special low prices**

For further details either call Customer Services on 01225 443400 or write to us at

Chivers Large Print Direct
FREEPOST (BA 1686/1)
Bath
BA1 3QZ